WHO STOLE
HALLOWEEN?

WHO STOLE HALLOWEEN?

MARTHA FREEMAN

SCHOLASTIC INC.
New York Toronto London Auckland Sydney
Mexico City New Delhi Hong Kong Buenos Aires

ISBN 0-439-88824-7

Published by Scholastic Inc., 557 Broadway, New York, NY 10012, by arrangement with Holiday House, Inc. SCHOLASTIC and associated logos are trademarks and/or registered trademarks of Scholastic Inc.

12 11 10 9 8 7 6 5 4 3 2 1   6 7 8 9 10 11/0

Printed in the U.S.A.   40

First Scholastic printing, September 2006

For my neighbors
in State College, Pennsylvania.
You are always an inspiration.

WHO STOLE HALLOWEEN?

Chapter One

Cats make excellent friends—except for one thing. They are bad explainers. Yasmeen says this is because a cat's whole vocabulary is only meow, purr, and hiss. She says meow, purr, and hiss are inadequate for good explanations.

Yasmeen is my best friend who happens to be a girl. She is smarter than me, but this time she's wrong. When he feels like it, my cat can tell me a lot with only a lazy blink or a quick swish of his tail. The trouble is that most of the time he doesn't feel like it.

The real reason cats are bad explainers is

simple: They are too impatient. The way a cat figures, if he understands something, you should understand it, too. And if you don't, then you are not worth his trouble.

I was thinking these thoughts on a gray and spooky October afternoon, the kind when the trees look sort of like skeletons and the shadows look like ghosts. Yasmeen and I were running side by side, chasing my cat, Luau.

So far, Luau had not bothered to explain where he was going or why, or whether we were supposed to follow him or what.

"What's your theory?" Yasmeen asked me. "What's he up to?"

Yasmeen is tall, skinny, and fast, while I am none of the above. I was struggling to keep up, gasping for breath. "I only hope . . . it's not over . . . to St. Bernard's," I said. "That place . . . gives me the creeps."

St. Bernard's is an old church near my street. Behind it is a just-as-old cemetery. I had hardly finished saying "the creeps" when Luau made a right turn and loped through the cemetery gate.

I swear, sometimes my cat has a nasty sense of humor.

Yasmeen laughed. "He's going to St. Bernard's all right." Then she ran ahead of me through the gate, warbling like some soprano werewolf, waving her arms over her head.

Being cool the way I am, I ignored her behavior. Unfortunately, I was so busy ignoring her behavior that I didn't see a broken headstone and I tripped.

"*Oh!* Oh, shoot—Alex, are you okay? Oh my gosh, you're bleeding!" Yasmeen had run back and knelt next to me. "I have Band-Aids," she said.

My hands hurt, but surprise stifled my tears. "You have Band-Aids?"

"I started keeping them in my pocket for emergencies," she said. "It's a crazy world, Alex. Anything might happen."

Yasmeen dabbed my scratches with antiseptic wipes—she had those, too—and smoothed on three Band-Aids. I expected Luau to be gone by the time she was done, but when I stood up,

I spotted him sitting by a statue of a grumpy-looking angel, washing his face.

"I don't get your feline," Yasmeen said.

"You don't think maybe he's doing his ace-detective thing again?" I asked.

Yasmeen grinned. "I hope so."

Luau seemed to be totally focused on personal hygiene, so, all sneaky, we crept toward him. We were about ten feet away when he looked up at us, which meant, *Oh, come on, guys— as if I didn't see you stalking me! I'm a* cat! *We invented stalking!*

Then he took one more swipe at his ear and bounded away.

Where was he going? It wasn't so long ago that my ace-detective cat had helped Yasmeen and me solve a mystery. Now he was so stuck-up he expected us to follow him anywhere, even into a deep, dark cemetery.

The wind made the dry leaves dance and rearranged the clouds. It also gave me goose bumps. Or was it being in a cemetery a week before Halloween that did that? Sometimes my imagination gets carried away. Everywhere Yasmeen and I ran, we were stomping on dead people, weren't we? And where there are dead people, there are ghosts and ghouls and zombies.

"There!" Yasmeen said. She stopped under an oak tree and pointed at Luau. By now, he had doubled back and was sitting next to a big, elaborate headstone beside the grumpy angel. It wasn't the stone that caught my attention, though. What I noticed was what was stuck to the back of it—some kind of flyer with a picture. Why would somebody attach a flyer to a head-stone, anyway?

Luau stretched and swished his tail and looked at us, which meant, *Why don't you read me what it says?*

If I had been by myself, I would have called Luau to come, then turned around and gone home. But Yasmeen was never going to let me get away with that. She just loves a mystery, the stranger the better. And guess what? The flyer on the gravestone was the start of another big mystery, one that would get me, and Yasmeen, and especially Luau into grave, grave trouble.

Chapter Two

Yasmeen was disappointed.

"A flyer posted on a gravestone—*that* would have been mysterious," she said. "But I guess it was only the wind holding it there. It must've blown through the fence or something."

She held the paper up. Under a photocopied picture of a sleek black cat were the words:

Please bring back Halloween!
Beloved pet, last seen October 22.
Call Kyle Richmond.
No questions asked!

Then there was a phone number and an address on Groundhog Drive.

"Isn't that near Ari's house?" Yasmeen asked me.

"Yeah," I said, "and I think I know Kyle from school—who he is anyway. Uh, can we go now?" The sun had sunk behind Mt. Lyon, and the light was fading fast. You can imagine how eager I was to be in a graveyard in the dark. "Come on, Luau. You ready?"

Luau side-rubbed my leg and looked up at me, which meant, *Can I have a ride, please? All that running has left me exhausted.* I picked him up and heaved him over my shoulder, which isn't as easy as it sounds. Luau is one of those big-shouldered, muscley cats. He's not fat, but he weighs a ton.

We started walking. Luau purred. Yasmeen lectured: "There's no such thing as ghosts, you know. They are merely figments of a vivid imagination."

Yasmeen talks like that a lot. Her mom is a librarian, and her dad is an English professor.

Her family lives next door to mine, so we've been friends since we were babies. It's only because I've had so much practice that I, a regular kid, can even understand her.

"That's your opinion," I said. "But plenty of people have seen ghosts. Plus there's that house on Main Street; everyone knows it's haunted."

By now we were walking back through the cemetery gate. The moon had come out, and three bats flitted overhead.

"The Harvey house?" Yasmeen shook her head. "Mr. and Mrs. Blanco bought that, did you know? I bet they never have seen any ghosts there—and neither have I."

Mr. and Mrs. Blanco live on the same street as Yasmeen and me, Chickadee Court. "Are the Blancos moving?" I asked.

"Uh-uh," Yasmeen said. "They didn't buy the house to live in. They're opening some kind of fancy store. My dad calls it a health boutique."

I laughed. "Makes perfect sense. A boo-tique!"

Yasmeen didn't laugh.

"It's a joke," I explained. "Ghosts? Boo?"

"I get it," Yasmeen said.

"Then you should have laughed," I said, "to be polite."

"Ha-ha," Yasmeen said.

"Thank you," I said.

Luau shifted his weight, and his whiskers tickled my ear. Only two blocks and we'd be home. My arms looked forward to putting him down. But Yasmeen had another idea. "Let's do some detecting," she said.

"No."

"Oh, come on," she said. "Just a teensy-weensy bit of detecting. *Harmless* detecting. I promise."

This was not a promise I could trust. And I definitely did *not* want to get involved in another mystery.

Still, I couldn't help but wonder what Yasmeen was thinking. So I asked her, and she answered with a question: "Didn't you notice something unusual about the flyer? Aside from its being on the gravestone, I mean. Here, look."

I studied the paper for a few seconds. "Well, the wording is kind of weird," I said. "What kind of kid says 'beloved'? Oh—and it doesn't say 'LOST.' Most flyers like this say 'LOST' at the top in big letters."

Yasmeen nodded. "Let's stop off at the address on the flyer—at Kyle's house," she said. "It's not that far. Let's ask him if there was something strange about the cat's disappearance. I don't know why exactly, but I have this funny feeling."

"What did you have for lunch?" I asked her.

"Ha-ha," she said.

Chapter Three

At Kyle's front door I shifted Luau on my shoulder and used my elbow to ring the bell. After a minute we heard footsteps inside, and then a boy older than Yasmeen and me answered. I recognized him from school, but Yasmeen asked, "Are you Kyle? From the flyer about the cat?"

The boy nodded. He was as tall and thin as Yasmeen, and he had brown eyes like hers, but his skin was as paper-pale as hers is cocoa-dark. He looked sad, and I wondered if he was sad about his cat or just sad in general.

"Halloween is a black cat," he said, "not an orange tiger like this guy. But thanks for trying."

It took a second before I realized Kyle thought we had found Luau and mistaken him for his own missing cat, Halloween. "We know this one's not yours," I said, "because he's mine. But my friend here—her name's Yasmeen—wants to ask you a couple of questions."

"We're detecting," Yasmeen said.

"*She* is detecting," I corrected. "I am holding the cat."

"Don't you go to my school?" Kyle asked.

"I'm Alex," I said, "in Mrs. Timmons' class. We live over on Chickadee."

"What do you want to know?" Kyle asked.

Yasmeen got right to the point. "You didn't put 'LOST' on the flyer. Was there a reason?"

Kyle nodded. "Halloween isn't lost. Someone stole her."

"That's terrible!" Yasmeen said.

Without thinking, I clutched Luau tighter. Then I forgot I wasn't detecting, and I asked, "How do you know?"

Before Kyle could answer, a little girl came running down the stairs behind him, only stopping when she crashed into his knees. *"Pow! Got you!"* she said to Kyle, then she looked up at us. "Who are . . . ? Hey, wait! I've seen you before. At school!"

"Not me," I said, but Yasmeen was nodding.

"Yup, I know you, too," she said. "You're Cammie. You go to preschool with my little brother."

Cammie smiled. "His name is Jeremiah. He is really weird."

Yasmeen nodded again. "Got that right."

"Why are you here?" Cammie asked.

"About Kyle's cat," Yasmeen said, "Halloween."

Cammie scowled. "Kyle is an old foo-foo head. He was *so mean*—"

"Mom!" Kyle hollered before Cammie could finish. When nobody answered, he said, "Excuse me a sec." Then he scooped up Cammie, who was wiggling and yelling, and carried her away.

"I'm sorry," he said when he came back. "She's, well . . . you know. Little kids."

Yasmeen said, "I know," but I didn't say anything because, actually, I don't know. Except for

Luau, I'm an only child, and cats never act crazy the way kids do. "Anyway," Yasmeen returned to being a detective, "are you sure somebody stole Halloween?"

"I'm sure," Kyle said, "because I saw it happen. It was late at night. Something woke me, and I looked out the window. I saw Halloween out here on the porch. There was a moon, but no other light. I couldn't see very well, but I definitely saw someone stroke Halloween and then grab her."

"Did you run after him?" I asked.

Kyle shook his head. "I wish I had, but I was so surprised and—I guess—scared."

"Was it a grown-up?" Yasmeen asked.

"I think so," Kyle said. "But I don't know for sure if it was a man or a woman or . . ."

Like I said, Kyle was pale in the first place. But now—was it my imagination? Or did he get even paler?

"Or what?" I asked.

Kyle smiled, but it was a sick, embarrassed smile. "You'll think I'm crazy," he said.

"Try us," Yasmeen said.

Kyle took a breath. "Or a ghost," he said.

Yasmeen and I looked at each other because, of course, we *did* think he was crazy. Kyle laughed a nervous laugh, then he shrugged and said, "It was dark."

"Whatever it was," Yasmeen said, "which way did, uh . . . *it* run with your cat?"

"Toward the cemetery, but I don't know after that. He was fast. Even if I had tried, I couldn't have caught him."

"Did you tell your parents?" Yasmeen asked.

Kyle nodded. "I woke them up, but they thought I was dreaming. They said, 'You just wait, she'll be home in the morning.'"

"Sounds like parents," I said. "Did you call the police?"

"My parents did," Kyle said. "A guy came. I don't remember his name exactly. Pickles or something."

"Officer Krichels," I said. I know all the police officers because my mom's one, too, a detective.

"That's it," said Kyle. "He wrote everything down, but it's not like he expected it to do any good. You could tell."

"That was Friday—yesterday?" Yasmeen said.

Kyle nodded. "Halloween's been missing since Thursday night."

"Has anyone phoned you?" I asked. "Anyone who saw the flyer, I mean?"

"No." Kyle looked sadder than ever. "Poor cat. She's a good one, too. She never hunts birds, only mice, and she always comes when I call. Plus she's funny. Her meow is all gruff and squeaky—like a rusty old hinge."

Kyle sighed, and for a second we stood there feeling sad together. Then out of nowhere Yasmeen said, "Don't worry, Kyle. We'll find your cat."

Kyle looked at us. "You *will*?"

I looked at Yasmeen. "We *will*?"

"Why did you tell him that?" I asked Yasmeen as soon as we were on the sidewalk.

"I couldn't help it, Alex," she said. "He looked so miserable."

"Not as miserable as he's gonna look when we don't find his cat!" I said.

"So we'll find his cat," Yasmeen said. "How hard can it be? We have a witness."

"Some witness," I said. "He thinks he saw a ghost! Besides, by now, how do we know the poor cat's even"—I put a hand over Luau's ears so he couldn't hear—"*alive*?"

Chapter Four

My shoulder was half-numb by the time I set Luau down at home. But did Luau even *mrrrf* his chauffeur a thank-you? He did not. Instead, tail in the air, he went to the kitchen to check out the action in his food dish.

Meanwhile, I could hear my parents upstairs. What were they laughing at, anyway?

"Hello?" I called.

More laughter. Then my dad answered, "Come on up, Alex. Get a load of your mom."

Luau followed me up the stairs to their bedroom. When I saw them, I thought they both had gone crazy. Mom was wearing what looked like black-and-white striped pajamas with a matching hat. Dad had on a police uniform that was too big for him. But the totally weirdest part was they were attached to each other with handcuffs.

"For once I'm the cop in the family," Dad said. "And she's my prisoner. Get it?"

"It was his idea," Mom said.

There is something freaky about seeing your parents in costume—like you want to ask, what happened to my *real* parents?

"You better go get ready, too," Dad said.

"Ready for . . . ? Oh!" Then I remembered the party. It made me feel better to realize *why* they were dressed up.

"The world's first-ever costume baby shower." Mom shook her head. "Leave it to Marjie Lee to come up with a harebrained idea—"

"Was it Marjie's idea?" Dad said. "I thought the hostess was that goofy friend of hers, the one that lives around the corner—what's her name?"

"You're probably right," Mom said. "Everybody calls her 'Miss' Deirdre because she teaches preschool. She's eccentric, but she's supposed to be a wonderful teacher. Anita Popp told me there's a waiting list to get into that school."

"I've never been to a baby shower," I said.

"They used to be women-only," Dad said. "But here in the new millennium, men and children have to go, too."

"*Have* to?" Mom repeated.

"*Get* to," Dad said quickly. "I meant *get* to."

"You mean just like here in the new millennium, women *get* to have careers?" Mom said.

Dad looked surprised. "You love your career," he said, "don't you?"

"Some days more than others," Mom said, "same as you love being home some days more than others."

"I had a good day," Dad said. "I did the grocery shopping, made the ears for Alex's costume, and fixed the leaky toilet in the downstairs bathroom. I guess your day wasn't so hot, though?"

"No, it sure wasn't," Mom said.

"What happened?" I asked her.

"Two missing cats," she said.

"You're kidding," I said, "because—"

Dad interrupted. "Is that all that went wrong?" he asked. "You seem pretty upset."

Luau bumped Dad's leg, which meant, *What could be more upsetting than missing cats?*

"It's not only the cats that got to me. It's where they were missing from." Mom paused, remembering something unpleasant. "I'll spare you the details, but it was a real strange coincidence. Two houses, opposite sides of town, but in both cases the cat owners seemed to me to be . . . how do I put it delicately? Negligent?"

"What's *negligent*?" I asked.

"Irresponsible. Like they didn't take such good care of their cats, didn't feed them well. I guess the bottom line is that they didn't seem like very nice people. And, I don't know, seeing animals treated badly? It's upsetting."

"How do you know they were bad cat owners?" I asked.

"There were other pets, too," Mom said. "A dog at one of the houses was chained to a tree—you could see its ribs, poor guy. At the other house there were some guinea pigs. . . ." Mom wrinkled up her nose. "Like I said, I'll spare you the details."

Dad said it seemed odd that people would call the police about cats they didn't even bother to care for properly. Mom was nodding. "I thought so, too," she said. "And if the cats had simply disappeared, neither owner would've bothered, I don't think. But the cats didn't just disappear. Both owners claim somebody sneaked onto their property at night, grabbed their cats, and ran."

"That's just what happened to Kyle who lives over on Groundhog!" I said, and then I explained about the flyer and visiting Kyle's house.

"You say Fred Krichels was already out there to talk to them?" Mom said. "Then I'd better sit down with him and compare notes. I hope it's not that Halloween business starting up again. I thought that old ghost story was forgotten by now."

"What old ghost story?" I asked, remembering what Kyle had said.

"Hey." Dad looked at his watch. "We don't have time for ghost stories—not if there's going to be any food left at the party. Alex, run along and get dressed. *Scoot!*"

All this time we'd been talking, Mom and Dad were still attached with the handcuffs. Now when Dad said "scoot," he made a sweeping motion that yanked Mom's arm along for the ride.

"Ow!" Mom said.

"Ow!" Dad rubbed his shoulder. "Uh, sorry."

"Give me the key," Mom said. "I still have to do my makeup."

"*You* have the key," Dad said.

"Since when does the prisoner keep the key?" Mom asked.

"Oh, come on," Dad jangled the handcuffs. "Stop clowning, honey, and unlock them."

Mom looked at him. "Me?" she said. "Clowning?"

Dad made a face. "Uh-oh."

Chapter Five

Our neighborhood is big on celebrations. We have a Christmas party and a Fourth of July picnic. We have an Easter egg hunt and a Passover dinner. We celebrate St. Patrick's Day and Chinese New Year.

And when there's something special like a new baby coming, there's a party for that, too.

The Lees live right next door—the other side from Yasmeen's family—but even so, we were late getting to their house. My parents hadn't found the handcuff key, and it took my mom a long time to do her makeup left-handed and attached to Dad. As we walked in the door they were both crabby and blaming each other.

Mrs. Ryan spotted them first and laughed. She was dressed like a little girl going to a party: short skirt, ankle socks, and a big bow in her hair. This made sense because Mrs. Ryan teaches first grade.

"Well, aren't you two *cute*?" she said. "Whose idea was it—don't tell me. Dan's? Am I right?"

Mom took a deep breath; Dad smiled an uncomfortable smile.

"What's wrong?" Mrs. Ryan said.

"Nothing," Mom said. "Everything is ducky."

"Noreen," Mrs. Ryan said to my mom, "I have known you for ten years, and something is much less than ducky. Wait a second—don't tell me—you've lost the key!"

I had to hand it to Mrs. Ryan. Not much gets past a first-grade teacher. Unfortunately, it did not improve my parents' mood when the next thing she did was crumple up in a laughing fit.

"Bill!" she called to her husband between cackles. "Come over here. You won't believe it!"

This was a bad time to hang out with my parents, so I aimed for the living room. The lights were dim there, and the whole place felt haunted. In the corners were gauzy spider-webs loaded with black plastic spiders. Fake bats dangled from the ceiling on elastic threads, so when you bumped them, they bounced. The food was creepy-looking, too: eyeball appetizers, hot dogs that looked like bloody fingers, Jell-O in the shape of a brain, a cake with a cardboard dagger stuck in it.

There were a lot of people around the food table, but Yasmeen was easy to spot. Her costume was bright yellow and black stripes; she was a bumblebee.

Before I could tell her about the two new cat-nappings, she frowned and said, "Okay, I give up. What are you supposed to be?"

"What do I look like?" I answered.

"A boy in orange sweat pants and an orange sweatshirt that doesn't exactly match, and you have two construction paper triangles on your head," she said.

I turned around and showed her my tail. "I'm Luau!" I said. *"Duh!"*

"Where are the claws?" Yasmeen said. "The sharp teeth? The intelligent expression?"

"Ha-ha," I said, and bit down on a taco chip.

Besides Yasmeen and Jeremiah and me, five other kids live on our street. There's Toby Lee, who is not quite three and about to be bugged by a new baby. There's Michael Jensen, who is rich and smart and, Yasmeen tells me, "really cute." There's Michael's little brother, Billy, who is always listening to his new iPod, so it's like he doesn't live here among us but in some other dimension. And there are the Sikora kids, Sophie and Byron. Sophie is the bad kid in the neighborhood, a year younger than Yasmeen and me, big for her age and spoiled. She can't walk into a room without breaking something, and she talks all the time. Her brother, Byron, is as quiet as wallpaper—I guess because Sophie has never let him talk.

All us kids were hanging out by the food, of course. Michael was dressed as Superman, and, wouldn't you know, Billy was a CD sandwich. His mom had covered two giant cardboard disks with foil, then suspended them on straps over his shoulders. I tried to tell him, "Good costume!" but he had his headphones on and couldn't hear me. Sophie was dressed as an angel, which had to be somebody's idea of a joke.

"You ought to see Mrs. Lee." Michael blew up his cheeks and stretched out his arms. "Her costume's a pumpkin, and she didn't have to use padding."

"Let's go," said Yasmeen.

The family room was crowded. Mrs. Lee sat in a big chair in the corner. Michael was right— she made a very convincing pumpkin. Next to her was her friend, Deirdre, the preschool teacher. Only she didn't look like her usual ditzy, cheerful self. She was wearing some kind of spooky gray costume with a gray wig and ghoulish black-and-gray face makeup. She was knitting with rainbow yarn.

"What do you think she's making?" I asked. "It sure is teeny."

"A sweater for the baby, I guess," Yasmeen said.

Somebody came up behind me and tapped my head with a big fist. I knew without turning around it was Bub.

"Hey," I said, and elbowed him in the belly. It was the easiest place because so much of Bub is belly.

"What's this in your hair?" he asked. "Oh, now I see, orange cat ears. You're supposed to be Luau, is that it?"

"I'm glad somebody understands," I said. Then I took a good look at him and laughed. Bub is an old guy who lives by himself at the end of our street. Some of the neighbors say he's original, and some of them say he's a slob. For the party he had dressed in red long johns, which are like old-fashioned one-piece pajamas that button up the front. He had a mask on, too, but he had pulled it up over his head, so I couldn't see what it was.

"What are *you* supposed to be?" I said.

He pulled the mask down over his face.

"You're a *fish?*" I said.

"I'm a red herring!" he said. Then he laughed and laughed.

In mystery stories a red herring is a clue that points to the wrong person. Bub loves mysteries. When he's not watching old mystery movies, he's reading old mystery books.

"What's he laughing at?" Yasmeen asked.

"Himself, as usual," I said.

"What've you been up to lately?" Bub asked me.

I told him about Kyle's missing cat, Halloween, and then I told him and Yasmeen what my mom had said—that two more cats were missing, too.

"Two more?" Yasmeen said. "Now we've got an even better mystery to solve!"

"Can't we leave it to the police?" I said. "My mom's a really good detective."

"And so are you," Yasmeen said. "It must be genetic."

I knew Yasmeen was buttering me up so I'd help her. Even so, it was nice, not to mention totally rare, to get a compliment from her. Meanwhile, Bub thought it would be great if Yasmeen and I went to work on another mystery, and he offered to help.

"Maybe you can," I said. "Mom said something about the missing cats being connected to a Halloween story. Do you know anything about that?"

Bub nodded. "I think I know what she's talking about. It has to do with the old Harvey house downtown, the one the Blancos put all that work into."

"The one that's *haunted*," I said, looking at Yasmeen.

"That's how the story goes," Bub said. "Supposed to be that the ghost has it in for cats—black cats in particular. It's been years now, but I can remember cats disappearing around Halloween time and the Harvey ghost taking the blame."

"There's no such thing as ghosts," Yasmeen said.

Bub shrugged. "I don't know if there is or there isn't. But if you want to know more about the story, we have an authority nearby—Jonathan

Stone. He was born here in town—knows where all the bodies are buried, so to speak."

Mr. Stone also lives on our street. He's an older guy. His wife is dead, and his kids are grown-up.

"Have you seen him tonight?" Yasmeen looked around.

Bub shook his head no. "He's not much for parties."

This was true. In fact, Yasmeen and I used to be afraid of him. But then last year when he caught us trespassing in his yard, he didn't yell, he invited us in, served us hot chocolate, and even gave us a really important clue to the mystery we were working on. That was the first one Luau, Yasmeen, and I solved, and it turned out to be pretty scary, as well as confusing. Somebody had been stealing pieces of our neighborhood's annual Twelve-Days-of-Christmas display.

"You know who else is missing tonight?" Bub asked. "The father."

It was my turn to look around. "Mr. Lee?"

"Ah-yup," said Bub. "I hear a business deal came up, and he's out of town."

This was no surprise. Mr. Lee works all the time, same as my dad did before he quit to be a househusband.

Now Miss Deirdre stood up and clacked her knitting needles to attract everyone's attention.

"Boys and girls?" she said. Then she looked all embarrassed and shook her head. "Sorry," she said. "It's force of habit. What I *meant* to say was welcome!"

She said a few more smiley words about the wonders of new babies and moms and all that. Then it was time for presents.

The first one was a baby monitor, one of those walkie-talkie things. You put the microphone by the crib so you can hear on the receiver if the baby fusses or burps or tries to escape. Bub had never seen one, so I explained.

Bub shook his head. "I never knew a baby that had trouble making itself heard."

Next, Mrs. Lee opened a tiny outfit with bears on it, and all the moms in the room said, *"Awww."* After that came a blanket with pictures of sailboats. Then another baby monitor. This one was what my dad would call high-tech, everything really small and shiny.

After a while, I learned something about baby showers: The presents are boring. About the only interesting one was a teddy bear that played music by Mozart. It came from Mr. and Mrs. Sikora, who explained that classical music makes babies smart.

"If that's true, they must have forgotten to plug in Sophie's bear," Yasmeen whispered.

I laughed, but Bub shook his head. "You kids are wrong about her. She's rambunctious, but she's smart as a whip. When my doorbell busted, who do you think rewired it?"

Yasmeen and I looked at each other. Was it possible Sophie was some kind of genius with electronic stuff?

Or maybe this was another one of Bub's famous jokes.

Anyway, after that, Mrs. Lee opened a battery-powered wastebasket for smelly diapers, and Yasmeen and I decided we couldn't take any more. Back in the living room, I dared her to eat one of the hot-dog fingers, but she couldn't, and it turned out neither could I. We took the dagger out of the cake instead, and shared a big piece.

"After church tomorrow," Yasmeen said, "we'll look for clues."

"I don't have time for detecting tomorrow," I protested. "I have homework."

Yasmeen ignored my argument. "The thief was in a hurry. People in a hurry drop things. I bet anything there's a clue. Don't worry," she said. "This case will be easy to solve. I swear."

Chapter Six

"So what are you proposing?" my mom asked my dad. We were home after Mrs. Lee's shower. Their door was closed, but I could hear them from the hallway. "Are we supposed to sleep like this?"

"Look at it this way," Dad said. "It's going to make a very funny story one day."

"Who would we tell?" Mom said. "Thanks to Beth Ryan, we're the laughingstocks of the neighborhood now!"

I knocked on their door.

"Come in," Dad said. When I did, I saw they

were standing as far apart as two people hand-cuffed together can stand.

"Can I help?" I asked.

"No," Mom said.

"Honey," Daddy said.

"Sorry," Mom said. "That wasn't fair. I'm not mad at you, Alex. I'm mad at *him*."

"Go ahead and look around," Dad told me. "It seems like we've eyeballed every cranny, but metal keys don't vaporize. It has to be somewhere."

Luau was right behind me, nose in the air like maybe he was trying to smell the key. I shook my parents' bedspread, opened bureau drawers, crawled around on the rug.

Luau, meanwhile, leaped onto my dad's bed-side table, sat down, and watched me. Then he pulled one of his favorite tricks, one he usually uses for waking me in the middle of the night. He batted things onto the floor. The alarm clock. Two books. A magazine. A seashell from our vacation last summer.

A key.

I reached down for it. "Does this look familiar?" I asked.

"The key!" Dad said.

Mom smiled. "Where was it?"

I took a deep breath and tried to speak in my best let's-all-remain-calm voice. "On your bedside table, Dad."

"I looked there!" Dad said.

"Well, you didn't look very hard," Mom said.

"Well, possibly if you hadn't been dragging me toward the bathroom so you could do your *makeup.* . . ."

I unlocked the handcuffs for them. They shook out their arms and rubbed their shoulders but never stopped arguing.

"You really must have your eyesight checked, Dan," Mom said. "You know, at your age—"

"*My* age?" my dad said. "You've got six months on me, Noreen."

Luau gave me a look that meant, *Cats have excellent eyesight, in case you didn't know.* Then he jumped to the floor and padded out the door toward my room. I followed.

"Good night, honey, and thanks!" my mom called.

"Yeah, Alex, thanks!" Dad called.

Don't thank me, I thought. Thank Luau.

The next day was Sunday. I slept late, ate my bagel and cream cheese, then played Lousy Luigi Brothers on the PlayCube. It was looking like pretty much a perfect day—the kind when you never get out of your pajamas—until Dad said, "Don't I remember something about math homework?"

And Mom said, "The day's half gone and you're not even dressed, Alex? You're squandering daylight!"

When Mom makes one of her "squandering daylight" speeches, resistance is futile. So I pulled on sweatpants and a T-shirt that didn't smell too bad.

The math homework turned out to be easy. When that was done and Yasmeen still hadn't called, I hoped that maybe she had forgotten all about detecting.

Yeah, right.

At three o'clock she knocked on the door.

"Sorry I'm late," she said.

"That's totally okay," I said.

"Mom and Dad were hosting the fellowship hour after church, so we had to clean up. It took forever. The people at our church can really put it away, that's what my dad says."

"It's probably too late to do any detecting now, right?" I said.

"What do you mean?" Yasmeen said. "There's plenty of light left. Come on. We'll go over to the cemetery and walk from there back to Kyle's house. Bring the ace detective, too. Since we're on the trail of a catnapper, he's going to want to help."

Chapter Seven

Yasmeen, Luau, and I have solved one whole mystery together. So I guess I can't claim to be an expert. But here is something I think I know. A lot of the time, solving mysteries is unexciting.

I mean, in the movies there are explosions and car chases and women wearing bathing suits. In real life it's more like you look around, you ask questions, and you think hard.

Anyway, unexciting is definitely how it was that Sunday afternoon. Yasmeen and I walked at the speed of snails from the cemetery gate to Kyle's house and back again. By the fence we found an empty beer can. On the sidewalk we found a gum wrapper. Next to an old green car we found a grocery receipt. Yasmeen, who was wearing yellow rubber gloves, carefully saved each in a plastic bag.

"What's with the gloves?" I asked her.

"So we can preserve the catnapper's fingerprints," she said.

"But we don't have a way to analyze fingerprints," I said.

"Your mom does."

"Right, Yasmeen," I said. "She's gonna get the whole FBI crime lab involved to find a missing cat."

"*Three* missing cats."

"We don't even know if the others are connected to this one!"

"Oh, come on, Alex. Do you think there's more than one thief grabbing cats in the middle of the night?"

"How do I know? Maybe it's a coincidence. Anyway, the circumstances in the other cases were different. My mom said those owners were negligent, didn't care that much about their cats. Does Kyle seem negligent to you?"

"No," Yasmeen admitted. "But that just makes it more mysterious, right?"

Luau did not turn out to be keen on detecting, even though the case was catnapping. What he wanted instead was regular napping, and the cemetery didn't disturb his dreams either. While Yasmeen and I collected our useless clues, he slept in a cozy spot by a headstone. We were about ready to give up when he strolled toward us, tail swishing, nose in the air.

"He smells something," I told Yasmeen.

"Does it have anything to do with Kyle's cat?" Yasmeen asked.

"More likely with some tasty rodent."

Luau sniffed for a few seconds, then he walked down the sidewalk and stopped next to the old green car. I could see he wanted to get under it from the curb, but the car was parked too close, so there wasn't space. He did a quick ear swipe and looked back at me, which meant, *Take a look under there, why don't you? Something smells* very *interesting.*

I crouched and peered into the darkness.

"What do you see?" Yasmeen asked.

"Nothing," I said, then, "Oh . . . wait. There is something. It's round." I reached and brushed it with my fingertips. "I need a stick—do you see one?"

What Yasmeen found was more like a branch. It was awkward, but I managed to bump it against the thing till I had moved it over to the side.

"Gloves!" Yasmeen said, but by then I had already grabbed the thing. Any catnapper prints were now mixed up with mine.

In daylight our mysterious object seemed to be a handkerchief wrapped around a ball of crinkly stuff. I held it up for Yasmeen to see. "It's a sachet," she said. "You know, you put them in drawers to make your clothes smell good."

Okay. But then why was Luau acting crazy—mewing pathetically and trying to climb me like a tree?

"Can he have it?" I asked.

Yasmeen said why not, so I tossed it on the

ground. Luau pounced, then looked around like he thought for sure someone must want to steal such a marvelous prize.

"No, really, Luau. It's all yours," I said. "Enjoy."

Luau is ordinarily a very dignified pet. But whatever this stuff was, it brought out his inner kitten. Clutching the ball between his paws, he rolled onto his back and thumped at it with his hind feet, finally tossing it into the air. Then—and I never knew he was this coordinated—he caught it in his mouth and rolled over and over with it till you'd swear he had to be dizzy.

And that's when—*duh*, Alex—I realized what the white ball was made of. I opened my mouth to say the word, but Yasmeen beat me to it: "Catnip!"

Chapter Eight

Was the catnip a clue?

Or a coincidence?

Yasmeen and I had a lot to discuss that night, so I got permission to eat over at her house. The only trouble with having dinner there is that her parents are so strict. Grace before dinner. Cloth napkins. And no matter what kind of mushy, mysterious green stuff a kid finds on his plate, he is expected to eat it.

"Alex?" Mrs. Popp, Yasmeen's mom, looked up at me after we'd all said amen. "Would you like to start the conversation?"

When I was little, Yasmeen's parents scared me. By now, though, I've figured out that they're okay, they even like me—as long as I remember to speak in complete sentences.

"Sure, Mrs. Popp," I said. "Yasmeen and I have had an interesting afternoon."

"Tell us about it, Alex," Yasmeen's dad said.

So—between small bites of some mysterious meat—I told them. In a way, it was nice to be telling the story now because for once Yasmeen didn't interrupt. At Yasmeen's house you don't dare interrupt.

". . . a sachet Yasmeen called it." I was almost done. "But then we both realized, because of how crazy Luau was acting, that it had to be cat-nip. After that, we brought it home. We're still trying to figure out what it means."

For about a minute Jeremiah, Yasmeen's little brother, had been shaking his head and looking gloomy. Actually, he looks gloomy most of the time.

"Do you have something to contribute, Jeremiah?" Yasmeen's mom asked.

"Uh-oh," said Jeremiah.

"Why do you say that?" asked Mrs. Popp.

"Because somebody's a litterbug," said Jeremiah. "Miss Deirdre tells us *never* be a litterbug. And I never will."

"Admirable, Jeremiah," said Professor Popp. "What else does Miss Deirdre tell you?"

"Put the play dough back in the bag or it will dry out," he said. "Drink your milk, unless you're allergic. Oh—and always be kind to animals. She says that a lot."

Professor Popp said, "Excellent advice," and he sounded serious, but he might have been kidding. Professor Popp has an English accent because he grew up on some island I can never remember; to me he always sounds serious.

Jeremiah nodded. "Miss Deirdre knows everything," he said.

"Everything?" asked Mrs. Popp.

Jeremiah nodded again.

"There's one thing I bet she doesn't know," Yasmeen said. "She doesn't know who stole Halloween."

"So you two children are at it again, eh?" said Professor Popp. "Playing detective? I must say I think the catnip is a clue. Could the thief have dropped it?"

"That's what I think," said Yasmeen. "The thief carried it so Halloween would like him—so she'd go with him and not complain."

"That's reasonable," said Mrs. Popp, "if we can associate the word *reasonable* with someone who steals cats. What kind of person would do such a thing?"

"A wacko!" said Jeremiah.

Professor Popp arched his eyebrows. "Jere*mi*ah?"

"Sorry," Jeremiah said. "A nut case?"

Mrs. Popp pursed her lips and shook her head.

This time Jeremiah thought for a few seconds. Then he said, "A lunatic."

His parents looked at one another. "Better," they agreed.

"Did you know the word *lunatic* comes from *luna*—the Latin word for moon?" Mrs. Popp asked. "A lunatic was thought to be somebody influenced by the moon."

"You mean like werewolves?" I asked.

Yasmeen laughed. "So now you think it was a werewolf who stole Halloween?"

Jeremiah shook his head again. "Uh-oh."

"You don't even believe in werewolves," I reminded Yasmeen, "or ghosts either."

"But ghosts are real," said Jeremiah, "aren't they?"

"No," said his mom.

"Possibly," said his dad. "You know, I've done a bit of research on ghost stories. Every culture has them. Is that coincidence?"

"Oh, Derek, for goodness sake," said Mrs. Popp. "When people don't understand something, they invent a supernatural explanation. There are many mysteries in the world, but one thing is certain: Ghosts exist *only* in the imagination."

Chapter Nine

There is something strange when you look into a mystery: It sort of takes over your brain and even your sleep. That night I dreamed we found a whole bunch of clues, but most of them turned into fish and swam away. The only one that didn't was a little slip of white paper with writing on it.

The dream woke me at six, and I couldn't fall back to sleep. Luau was awake, too, lying on my feet, blinking at me and purring, which meant, *I love you, Alex, I love you so—especially when you give me catnip.*

Down the hall I could hear my mom in the

shower. It was Monday. She worked an early shift. This would be my best chance to talk to her.

I went down to the kitchen and poured myself a bowl of Pirate Berry Crunch. Mom came down a couple of minutes later. When she saw me, she jumped.

"What on earth are you doing up?" she asked.

"Sorry," I said. "I couldn't sleep."

The coffeemaker was burbling. Dad measures out the grounds and water the night before, then sets a timer so it's ready when Mom gets up. I used to think this was nice of him, but Mom says he only does it so he can sleep in without feeling guilty. Now she poured herself a mug and sat down across from me at the table.

"Is something wrong?" she asked.

"Just the missing cats," I said. "I can't stop thinking about them—Kyle's especially." Then I told her about my dream and about finding the catnip under the car. I told her what Bub said about a ghost story, too.

Mom nodded. "We've been lucky the last few years. No cats stolen at all. But before that, I remember several incidents. People with a sick sense of humor stole them and blamed the ghost. Once there was a ransom note. Another time somebody deposited two in the cellar at the Harvey house. It was vacant then. Luckily, the cats made plenty of noise, and a neighbor heard them. The cats were pretty hungry by the time we found them."

"Kyle said the thief might have been a ghost," I told her.

Mom laughed and shook her head. "Right, honey. And the tooth fairy robs banks in her off-hours."

I laughed, too. Then I told her Mr. Stone was supposed to be the expert on the old ghost story.

Mom said that didn't surprise her, then she looked at her watch and stood up. "I've got a seven o'clock meeting. We're planning our patrols for Halloween night."

"But you haven't eaten breakfast," I protested.

"There'll be doughnuts at the meeting."

"You won't let *me* eat doughnuts for breakfast," I pointed out. "You say they're bad for me."

"I'm right, too," she said, "as usual." She put her mug in the dishwasher, then ducked into the downstairs bathroom. When she came out, her police uniform was buttoned up and her lips were pink.

"Go get 'em, Mom," I said.

"I will, honey." She started down the hallway to the garage, then paused. "What's Kyle-over-on-Groundhog's last name?" she asked.

"Richmond," I told her.

Mom nodded. "I'll talk to Fred Krichels today, take a look at his report. It seems likely the catnapping incidents are related, don't you think? And maybe you and Yasmeen could get Mr. Stone to tell you that ghost story. Who knows? It might help us solve the case."

I was surprised, and kind of flattered, that Mom had asked for our help. "Sure," I said. "So you don't mind if Yasmeen and I try to find Kyle's cat?"

Mom smiled. "I don't mind," she said. "But this time, Alex, *please* be more careful. No death-defying midnight runs through the neighborhood. Deal?"

"Cross my heart," I said.

Chapter Ten

Dad came down about fifteen minutes later. I was clean and dressed and full of cereal. I was reading the sports section. Dad was as surprised as Mom, but he didn't jump. Instead, he asked about my spelling test.

"Oh, *no!*" I said. "I was going to study last night, but then I went to the Popps. . . . Do we have time to go over the words?"

"Hand me the list," Dad said.

I pulled it out of my backpack. Dad held it close to his face, then he stretched out his arms and held it far away. He opened his eyes wide. He squinted.

"Can't you read it?" I asked.

"Of course I can read it," he said. "First word: *glamorous.*"

"*Glamorous?*" I shook my head. "That's not one of our words."

"Sure it is," said Dad. "I mean"—he moved the paper away again—"I think it is."

I took the list back. "Dad, the word is *generous.*"

Dad shrugged. "*Glamorous, generous*—the rule is the same: *O* before *U* except after moo."

"Ha-ha, Dad." I slid the list into my backpack. Yasmeen could quiz me on the way to school.

Dad frowned and rubbed his eyes. "Maybe I should make that phone call after all," he said.

"To the eye doctor you mean?"

"Oh, no." Dad shook his head. "I don't care what your mom says, it's not serious enough for an M.D. But Eric Blanco's got that new store downtown, I think I told you? It's one of those health-organic-type stores. Five-dollar zucchinis, tea bags from Tibet, vitamin Q. . . ."

"In the Harvey house," I said. "Mom and I were just talking about that place. But I don't understand. What do five-dollar zucchinis have to do with your eyes?"

"Oh, it's probably a lot of hooey," Dad said. "But Eric claims he's got some miracle pills—vitamin A it must be. He says if I take them, my eyesight will be as good as Luau's."

I couldn't believe my dad. Miracle pills? Why didn't he just get glasses like all the other old people?

"You know Eric sells pumpkins, too," Dad said. "Organic, homegrown, all that stuff. What do you say we go over there before dinner? I've got that PTA meeting, but after that we could go get the raw materials for our jack-o'-lantern."

"Can Yasmeen come?" I asked.

"Sure," Dad said, "and speaking of Yasmeen . . ."

She was knocking at the front door, same as she does every day. That meant it had to be precisely 7:45. Yasmeen is never late to pick me up for school.

"Want to come pumpkin shopping with us?" Dad asked her.

"At the haunted house," I added.

Yasmeen said probably—she'd have to check with her dad. Then she adjusted the straps on my backpack, and we headed out the door.

It is a two-block walk from my house to College Springs Elementary School—one block to Bub's at the end of Chickadee Court and one along Groundhog Drive to the school. For the first block I filled Yasmeen in on what my mom had said about stolen cats and how Mom wanted us to get the ghost story from Mr. Stone. For the second Yasmeen quizzed me on spelling words. We are in different rooms this year, so we figured we'd meet at lunch to plan our next move.

But our next move came to us.

Yasmeen and I had just sat down in the cafeteria when Kyle came over to our table. We were shocked. At our school it's strange for a kid in a higher grade to talk to a kid in a lower one. It's more than strange, it's like totally uncool for a kid in a higher grade to risk this at lunch—when his friends are bound to see.

Whatever Kyle wanted, it had to be really important.

"Uh . . . I came to ask you . . . ," he began, and if it's possible, he looked more miserable than before, ". . . uh, I mean, everything's okay now. . . . You don't need to get my cat back."

Chapter Eleven

Yasmeen dropped her sandwich she was so surprised. Me—I almost choked on my Chips Ahoy!

"What?" Yasmeen said. "She came back on her own, you mean?"

Kyle shook his head no. "I wish, but that's not it. I'm just saying—of course I *want* her back. She was like my best friend . . . but I don't want you to help get her for me."

"Why not?" I said. "We already found out some stuff."

"What?" Now Kyle looked scared. "What have you found out?"

"Nothing," Yasmeen said.

I looked at her. "*Nothing*? That's not—"

Yasmeen interrupted me with a kick. While I rubbed my shin and tried to figure out what I was missing, she said, "Nothing that was any help. Don't worry about it, Kyle. If you don't want me to bring your cat back, I won't."

Kyle was already standing up and looking around—wondering which of his friends had seen him and how much he was going to suffer for talking to us.

"Thanks," he said. "I appreciate it. I know maybe it seems weird, but . . ." He shrugged, turned, and walked away.

When he was out of earshot, I let Yasmeen have it. "What was that about? I hope you're carrying your famous Band-Aids because I need one where you *assaulted* me!"

"I didn't hurt you," Yasmeen said, then she thought again. "Did I? Roll up the leg of your jeans and let me look."

"Oh, right, Doctor Popp," I said. "In the middle of the cafeteria at lunchtime, I'm going to show you my shin."

"Suit yourself," she said, and took a bite of

her sandwich. Meanwhile, our friend Russell came over and sat down. He had a tray full of cafeteria delights.

"What is that?" Yasmeen asked him.

Russell took a bite. "I'm not sure, but it tastes good. Hey—that was a hard spelling test, huh? I think I got 0 out of 20."

Actually, I had thought the test was okay. But it would sound like bragging to tell Russell that now. And with him here, Yasmeen and I couldn't really talk about the missing cats either. So instead, we acted like regular, normal, everyday kids— instead of hardworking detectives—and talked about regular, normal, everyday stuff like trick-or-treating and kickball and video games.

In class after lunch we had time to work on our relief maps of Mexico. While I mixed up the dough ingredients and stirred the paint, I thought about poor Kyle and his missing cat and his strange request. I also tried to figure out how come Yasmeen had kicked me. I mean, she wanted to shut me up, but why?

Anyway, it wasn't so smart to think about the case while I worked, because the dough came out all runny and my green paint looked blue. Mrs. Timmons asked me if I was feeling okay and even put her hand on my forehead like maybe I had a fever. Mrs. Timmons likes me because we have cats in common. She has a white one with blue eyes and an orange tiger like Luau, which is something everyone in our room knows because she is always brushing white and orange fur off her clothes.

"Don't forget to put your dough away in a Ziploc," she reminded the class when we were done working. I smiled because it made me think of Miss Deirdre and Jeremiah's preschool. I guess when it comes to dough, you never grow up.

Yasmeen met me at the door of the classroom after school.

"There was something strange about the way Kyle was talking," she said. "Did you notice? He was so nervous."

I slung my backpack over my shoulders, and we started walking down the hall. "Sure, I saw he was scared," I said. "So what, though? Why not tell him about the catnip? Why not tell him what my mom said?"

"I don't know how to explain this," she said, "but something told me not to trust him—like an instinct."

We walked out the front door of the school and into the daylight. It was a perfect fall afternoon—blue sky, white clouds, fiery leaves.

"Come on, Yasmeen," I said. "You don't think he stole his own cat, do you?"

Yasmeen shook her head like she was trying to straighten out her thoughts. "That doesn't make sense, does it?" she said. "But wait. What about this? What if he made up the story about seeing the thief?"

"And he doesn't want us to do any detecting because he's afraid we'll find out," I said.

Yasmeen nodded. "Exactly."

"But why would he do that?" I asked.

"Maybe something else happened to Halloween," Yasmeen said. "Maybe Halloween wasn't supposed to go outside, and Kyle let her out, and she got hit by a car or something else bad, and now Kyle is afraid he'll get in trouble."

That was a pretty smart guess, I thought. Lots

of people keep their cats inside to protect them. I could imagine a kid inventing a story to stay out of trouble and then getting scared someone would find out.

But I would never tell Yasmeen I thought she was smart. She already thinks she is plenty smart. So I just said, "Yeah, maybe. Anyway, now we'll never know for sure."

"What do you mean?" Yasmeen asked.

"You told Kyle we would quit detecting," I said.

Yasmeen shook her head and grinned. "No, I didn't."

I thought back to what she had said in the cafeteria. "You told him you wouldn't bring Halloween back," I said.

Yasmeen nodded. "But I never said *you* wouldn't."

Chapter Twelve

Yasmeen and I had just turned the corner onto Chickadee Court when we spotted a police car parked in front of Bub's house.

That sounds scary.

But it wasn't.

There's a police car there a lot. Officer Krichels is Bub's friend. He likes to stop off for soup.

I looked at Yasmeen. "Are you thinking what I'm thinking?"

She nodded. "We need to talk to Officer Krichels. But what time are we going to get the pumpkins?"

"Dad said the PTA meeting will go till five," I said.

Yasmeen smiled. "I can be a little late getting home, too. My dad won't be back with Jeremiah till four."

A minute later, Bub opened the door for us and bowed. "*Bienvenue,* Madame, Mess-yer. Zee potage of zee day eez vee-shee-swaz." He was speaking in a French accent that even I knew was a bad French accent. It cracked us up. "Zat just means zee zoup de po-tay-toe. Eet's zupposed to be cold, but who likes zee cold zoup? I serve my vee-shee-swaz fresh from zee stove."

"Sounds great," I said, "Mess-yer."

Bub brought Yasmeen and me bowls of white soup sprinkled with flakes of green stuff. Officer Krichels was just getting ready to leave.

"Can we ask you something?" I asked him.

"Your mom told me you were interested in the missing cats," he said. "It's a bad time of year for it, you know. Better keep a close eye on Luau."

Yasmeen said, "Did you notice anything odd about Kyle, the kid you talked to on Groundhog Drive?"

Officer Krichels scratched his chin. "Can't say I did. Kind of a Gloomy Gus, but his cat was gone, so who could blame him? Now, that pip-squeak sister o' his, *she* was somethin'."

"Did she say anything?" Yasmeen asked.

"The pip-squeak?" said Officer Krichels. "You couldn't shut her up! I didn't pay much attention on account of how she wasn't a credible witness. That means someone you can believe."

Officer Krichels is nice, but he treats all kids like they're two years old. Sometimes, like now, Yasmeen gets impatient.

"I *know* what a credible witness is," she said. "Do you remember *anything* the little sister told you?"

Officer Krichels had his hand on Bub's door-knob. "Bunch o' nonsense. Something about how her rotten big brother tortured the cat. . . ." Officer Krichels shrugged. "You know siblings—they're always out to get each other."

Officer Krichels saluted Bub. "Great soup today, like always."

Bub was sitting at the table with us, his hands clasped over his belly. He nodded at his friend, "See ya tomorrow. I'm thinkin' black bean."

The instant the door closed, Yasmeen burst. *"I cannot believe him!"*

"Yasmeen," I said, warning her.

But Bub just laughed. "One of the sweetest guys I know," he said, "but genius is not one of his attributes."

"I suppose now we should talk to Kyle's little sister," I said, "to Cammie."

Yasmeen picked up her soup bowl and gulped the last bit. "I don't see how we can do that," she said, "without Kyle finding out we're still detecting."

It was getting close to four. Yasmeen went to call her dad and ask if she could go with Dad and me to the Harvey house to get pumpkins. I told Bub the whole story, and to my surprise he picked up right away on something my mom had mentioned.

"Ransom note," he repeated. "I bet you dollars to doughnuts Kyle got a ransom note.

It happens all the time in books. The detectives are working their tails off, and suddenly whoever it was hired 'em calls and tells 'em to quit. In this case, the catnapper told Kyle not to try to find his cat, just pay the money. That's why Kyle talked to you today. That's why he looked so scared."

Chapter Thirteen

Mr. and Mrs. Blanco must have worked really hard to fix up the Harvey house because it hardly even looked haunted anymore. The paint was fresh, and the twisted rungs of the black metal fence by the sidewalk had been straightened out. All the little frame-doodads around the porch and windows had been repaired and nailed back into place. From the sidewalk I could see for the first time that this pretty much used to be a mansion compared with the other houses on Main Street. I guess it was built by somebody rich.

Yasmeen, my dad, and I opened the gate—

which didn't even squeak—and walked through the front yard toward the porch. There were pumpkins on either side of the walk. The house was brightly lit, and there was a new purple sign:

HARVEY HOUSE HEALTH BOUTIQUE
NATURAL FOODS AND FIBERS, VITAMINS,
AND HOMESPUN REMEDIES
EVERYTHING FOR YOUR GOOD HEALTH

"What's a homespun remedy?" I asked.

Dad scratched his head. "Eric Blanco explained the theory to me on the phone," he said, "but to tell the truth, I don't get all of it. The gist seems to be that sometimes weaknesses can be repaired through the 'introduction of offsetting substances.'"

Yasmeen and I looked at each other. *Huh?*

Dad laughed. "Let's say you want to build muscles. The homespun idea would be that you swallow a tonic made from something strong— like an ox."

"You mean drink ox blood?" I shuddered. "I think I'd rather do push-ups."

"I'm not much for push-ups," Dad said. "And who knows? Maybe it works."

Mr. Blanco met us at the front door of the store. "Welcome, neighbors!" he said, then he looked at Dad. "You here for my eyesight pills?"

Dad smiled. "Frankly, I'm still skeptical. But we know for sure we're in the market for pumpkins."

"We've got plenty of pumpkins," Mr. Blanco said, "and all of them certified organic. You kids want to pick out a couple of good ones while the old fogies talk?"

Yasmeen and I went back out into the yard to look at the selection. I am not a big shopper. Right away I noticed a pumpkin that was more or less round and pretty big. It didn't have any rough brown places or dots, either.

"This one's good," I said.

Yasmeen examined it. "It has a big green spot," she said.

"Only on one side," I said. "We can cut it out for the nose or something."

Yasmeen said she was going to keep looking,

which meant picking up every single pumpkin, turning it over and over, then shaking her head and setting it back down.

"Do you think Bub's right?" I asked her, "about the ransom note?"

"But what about what Officer Krichels told us?" Yasmeen said. "Maybe Kyle was afraid we would find out that he tortured his cat, and that's why he called us off."

"I think the ransom note is more likely. To me it seems like Kyle really liked that cat."

Yasmeen had picked up a small pumpkin and now held it under her arm. "What about this? The catnapper was misinformed. He thought Kyle loved his cat enough to pay ransom, but he didn't really."

My head was spinning, which is precisely what I don't like about detecting—too much brain work. I nodded at the pumpkin Yasmeen was holding. "Is that the one you want?" I asked.

"It's perfect," she said.

I thought it was way too small, but I didn't want to encourage more shopping. "You're absolutely right," I said.

A thump on the porch startled me, but it was only Dad. He held up a bag for me to see. "You'll never believe it," he said. "Organic marshmallows!"

"Are regular marshmallows *in*organic?" Yasmeen asked.

"Got me," said Dad. "I'm just telling you what it says on the bag. Why don't you take these over to Mr. Stone? He's the one who loves marshmallows, right?"

"Served with hot chocolate," I said, "and a ghost story."

The sky had been clear a minute ago, but now I felt a gust of cold wind and heard a rumble like thunder.

Dad checked the sky, too. "Weather looks iffy all of a sudden," he said. "Let's take your pumpkins in and pay up."

Yasmeen followed me into the Harvey house. It was bright and cheery inside, with hand-painted signs, bins of vegetables and grains, shelves of vitamin-type bottles, a rack of spices and herbs in little plastic bags, books, and a cold case with yogurt and juices. The cash register was behind a counter near the door. On the counter was a basket of white things that re-minded me of Luau's catnip sachet. I was about to inspect one when Mr. Blanco said, "That will be forty-two dollars and ninety-seven cents, Dan."

I said, "For pumpkins and marshmallows?"

"*And* eyesight pills," Mr. Blanco said.

Dad handed over his credit card. "For that price, they'd better work," he said.

Mr. Blanco smiled. "As I explained, this is just enough for a few days, Dan. I'll call when I get a fresh batch."

Yasmeen said how nice the store was, and Mr. Blanco thanked her. Then I asked about the ghost. Did he know the house was supposed to be haunted?

Before Mr. Blanco could answer, I heard a throaty howl that seemed to come from every direction at once. I gave Yasmeen a What-the-heck? look, and the next thing a flash of light turned her face all eerie blue, sick, and scared. The gust of wind, the howl, the flash—and sud-denly a *crack* like thunder splitting a tree trunk an inch from my ear . . . then a sizzle of electricity, and everything went black.

Chapter Fourteen

I held tight to my pumpkin, like it might turn out to be some kind of protection from supernatural forces. My dad put his hand on my shoulder. "Alex? Yazzie?" Even with him there, I could feel my heart pounding and hear Yasmeen breathing fast, like she was scared.

The next sound in the dark was Mr. Blanco. He was *laughing* and at the same time rustling around behind the counter. *"There,"* he said, and a lantern came on. "Sorry about that, Dan . . . , kids," he said. "It happens now and again. I think it's that same ghost you were asking about, Alex."

"You're kidding," said Dad. "Aren't you?"

Mr. Blanco bent down and fooled with some switches behind him on the wall. After a few seconds the overhead lights blazed back on. He turned toward us again and shrugged. "Tell you the truth, I don't know if I'm kidding. All I know is this is the fourth time it's happened just that way—wind, howl, flash, thunder, and out go the lights. It's a bother, but it doesn't seem to be dangerous. The only trouble is it scares the customers—some customers."

"I'm not scared," Dad said, but I noticed his face looked whiter than usual.

"I am!" I said.

"You don't really believe in ghosts, do you?" Yasmeen asked Mr. Blanco.

"Seems like it's more that the ghost believes in *me*," said Mr. Blanco. "Besides, have you got a better explanation?"

Yasmeen usually has all the answers. Now she opened her mouth like she was going to fill us in, but then she closed it again. "No," she said. "I don't."

* * *

At home there was a message on the answering machine. It was from Billy Jensen telling us that Marjie Lee had had a baby girl at six that morning. It might seem weird that a first-grader would be making that kind of phone call, but in our neighborhood it made total sense. Billy Jensen loves to spread news.

I told Dad about the baby, then I phoned Mr. Stone to ask if he would tell us the famous ghost story.

"Oh, you kids aren't interested in an old chestnut like that," he said.

Mr. Stone can be what my dad calls "difficult" and my mom calls "ornery."

"We really *do* want to hear it, Mr. Stone," I persisted. "Oh—and I forgot to mention, Dad bought you a bag of fancy marshmallows, too. They came from Mr. Blanco's new store downtown."

"A present for *me*?" Mr. Stone said, and I could hear the smile in his voice. "Tomorrow after school then. Three-thirty? I'll make hot chocolate."

Dad called me for dinner as soon as I hung

up. I sat down at the table in the kitchen and poured myself a glass of milk. Luau sauntered in and glanced at his food dish in the corner. No luck there, so he decided to check out my food dish—my dinner plate, I mean. He jumped into an empty chair and peeked over the edge of the table. He was hoping for fish sticks or tuna casserole, but we were having macaroni-and-cheese from a box with a side of sliced apple.

Luau swished his tail a couple of times and looked at me, which meant, *I never cease to be amazed at the strange foods you humans eat.* Then he stepped into my lap, circled, and curled up for a nap.

Dad had just served his own plate when we heard the whir and squeak of the garage door opening. "Glory be." Dad looked at his watch. "Mom's home early."

Two sticky bites later, she walked into the kitchen looking tired.

"Another bad day?" Dad asked her.

Mom nodded and sank into a chair. Dad popped up and got her a plate of food. Mom thanked him, but didn't eat. Instead, she rested her head on her hand and stared at her macaroni.

"What happened?" I asked her.

She didn't look up. "Two more missing cats."

"Really?" I shifted my legs, which woke Luau. "Then I'd better call Yasmeen."

Dad put his hand on my shoulder. "Detecting can wait, Alex. It's rare that we're all together."

Mom insisted she wasn't hungry, but Dad folded his arms across his chest and said, "Noreen, I want you to eat that macaroni—every bite!"

Mom sampled a single elbow, then two, then finally a regular forkful. Soon her macaroni was gone, and Dad brought her a second serving.

"I guess I forgot to eat today—after my doughnut breakfast, that is," Mom said.

"Well, no wonder you're a basket case." Dad put her plate back in front of her. "And eat your apple, too, honey. It's good for you."

"I don't like apples," Mom said.

"Oh, for heaven's sake," Dad said, "*everybody* likes apples."

I thought of something—not about apples, about cats. "Were these cats taken from 'negligent' owners, too?"

Mom nodded. "Pretty bad."

"Did the owners see the thieves?"

"One was asleep. The other thought she saw . . ." Mom shook her head.

"Saw what?" I asked.

"Thought she saw a ghost. Honestly, some of the people in this town. They are *so* superstitious."

"But, Mom," I said, "that's what Kyle said, too. I don't know. Maybe . . . ?"

Mom looked at me. "Sweetheart, I have enough to worry about putting bad *people* in jail. If I have to worry about bad ghosts, too, well . . . I'll be seeking a new line of work."

Mom sounded so exhausted that I didn't want to ask her anything else. "Yasmeen and I are going to get the whole ghost story from Mr. Stone tomorrow," I said.

"That's good, honey," Mom said. "If this is all a Halloween prank, maybe it will shed some light. So far, though, I don't see a connection to the Harvey house."

"Speaking of the Harvey house," Dad said, and he told Mom about buying the pumpkin and the lights going out. I noticed he didn't say anything about his new pills, so I didn't say anything either.

Full of macaroni, Mom cheered up some and asked if there was anything new with Yasmeen's and my detecting. If I told her we were annoyed with Officer Krichels for not listening to Kyle's little sister, she would think I was dissing a fellow police officer. So instead, I stuck to what Kyle said in the cafeteria and how Bub thought maybe Kyle had received a ransom note.

"Ransom note?" she said. "Hmmmm. Then I guess maybe tomorrow I should go on over to Kyle's house myself. Fred Krichels might have missed something."

"That is a really, *really* good idea," I said.

Chapter Fifteen

After dinner, Dad and I planned to carve the jack-o'-lantern. When I stood up I deprived Luau of his bed, also known as my lap. So Luau would forgive me, I put a cat treat on the floor for him. Luau watched it for a few seconds. It didn't move, so he sneaked up to it, wiggled his rump, and pounced.

Dad shook his head. "For a cat who is so smart sometimes, he sure is stupid other times."

We talked about school while Dad got out newspaper, a big spoon, a marker, a carving knife, a paring knife, and a bowl—in other words, jack-o'-lantern tools. My job was the gooshy one—scoop out the seeds and the stringy orange crud, and then put them in the bowl. Boy, was I glad to wash my hands when that was done.

"Scary or funny this year?" Dad asked me.

"Funny," I said, and I drew a face that had extra-wide nostrils. That way I'd be sure to cut out all of the green spot. While I was drawing, Mom came in. She was wearing ratty pink sweats and the fuzzy slippers I had given her for her birthday. Sometimes I wonder what bad guys would think if they saw her like that.

"Can I help?" she asked.

"You can separate the seeds from the goop," Dad said, "so we can roast them."

Mom poked the contents of the bowl with her fingertip and made a face. "How come I always get the glamour jobs?"

Dad kissed her cheek and said, "Because you are such a glamour-puss."

Mom rolled her eyes, but then she went ahead and dunked her hands into the bowl and started picking out seeds. Meanwhile, Dad and I took turns using the paring knife to carve the face. When we were done, we lit the stumpy little candle inside the jack-o'-lantern and turned off the lights.

"*Oooooh,*" Mom said, like she does every year. "We have two real *artists* in the family."

"Thanks, honey." Dad put his arm around her.

"Can we put him on the front step now?" I asked.

Dad shook his head no. "Halloween's Friday," he said. "You can wait four days."

Walking to school the next morning, Yasmeen and I came to a significant conclusion about who stole Halloween: We didn't have the faintest idea.

Was it the same person who stole the other four cats?

Did Kyle make the whole thing up?

Was there a ransom note like Bub thought?

Yasmeen said we only knew one thing for sure: Ghosts had nothing to do with it.

I didn't tell her, but I wasn't even positive about that.

*   *   *

School did nothing to cheer us up. We hardly said a word on our way to Mr. Stone's house that afternoon. Inside, I pulled the fancy organic marshmallows out of my backpack. They were slightly smooshed after spending so much time with my math book and my social studies binder.

Mr. Stone smiled. "Thank you, Alex. And be sure to thank your dad, too. Let's try them right out, shall we?"

I could smell the hot chocolate on the stove.

Mr. Stone's house is pretty big, and he has lived there all by himself since his wife died. Most of the house seems kind of cold and deserted, but the kitchen is warm. That's where Yasmeen and I always sit when we visit.

Now he poured a mug of hot chocolate for each of us. "You kids don't really want to hear—" he began.

I cut him off. "We *do* really want to hear."

"My mom told me that this is a story from your childhood," Yasmeen said.

"Gracious, Miss Popp, how old does your mother think I am?" Mr. Stone said. "This story comes from my *grandfather's* childhood. It was my grandfather who told my dad and my dad who told me." Mr. Stone shifted in his chair like Luau does when he's settling in for a while. He took a sip of cocoa.

"My father," he said, "was a minister, accustomed to giving sermons, and he had quite the flair for the dramatic, something I fear that I lack. Every year at Halloween he'd gather us kids around and start this story the same way: 'Wisps of cloud obscured the moon that Halloween night, the night old man Harvey met his maker, murdered by his very own cat.'"

Chapter Sixteen

Yasmeen and I looked at each other, then spoke at the same time: "His *cat*?"

Mr. Stone nodded. "A big cat, black as midnight, with eyes as green and bright as emeralds. A smart cat, too! He was known throughout the town for his intelligence. One time a child fell through the ice, and the cat stayed on the bank howling till someone came to the rescue. Another time Mrs. Harvey couldn't find her diamond necklace—the Harveys were the richest people in town—and who led her directly to it? That big black cat."

"But why would a cat want to murder its owner?" I asked. I admit I was thinking of Luau. He's smart, too. Didn't he find the key to the handcuffs? Maybe he was a descendant of Old Man Harvey's cat. Maybe I should watch my back.

Mr. Stone continued: "The way my dad told it, Old Man Harvey was rich for three simple reasons: He worked hard. He was greedy. And he was mean. The only person he cared about was Marianne Harvey, his wife. Supposedly, she was a great beauty, and he wooed her for a long time, showering her with extravagant gifts like that necklace. Her sister—she married my grandmother's cousin—always said that Marianne got married against her better judgment. She was finally so sick of being pestered that she said yes. Besides, in those days a girl didn't have so many options."

Mr. Stone took more marshmallows from the bag and put them in our mugs. "The scary part's coming," he said. "You'll need your strength. Now, as I was saying, Mr. Harvey adored his wife and didn't give a fig about anybody else."

"How did he feel about his cat?" I asked.

Mr. Stone looked at me. "I am pretty sure, Mr. Parakeet, that when my dad used to tell this story, we kids didn't ask questions."

"Sorry," I said.

"Well, one day—it was in October, not so very long before Halloween—Mr. Harvey didn't come in to work. Now, I know you're going to ask, Mr. Parakeet, so I'll go ahead and tell you: Mr. Harvey owned a dry goods store, the first in College Springs, and it was unlike the old miser to miss a workday. Along about noon one of his employees, a fellow by the name of Floyd, went to the house to check up on him.

"Floyd rang the bell. No answer. Floyd knocked on the door. No answer. Floyd called out." Mr. Stone looked at us.

"No answer!" Yasmeen and I chorused.

Mr. Stone nodded. "That's right. Now Floyd was worried. He probably ought to have run for the authorities. But he was a strong and steady fellow, and he decided first to have a look around on his own. As luck would have it, the parlor window was open a crack, and Floyd wedged his fingers under, pushed the window up, and climbed inside."

Mr. Stone paused and shook his head mournfully. I wanted to ask about ten questions—like how old was Floyd? and where was the dry goods store?—but I clamped my lips together and kept quiet.

"Well," Mr. Stone sighed, "*what* a sight in that parlor, that same parlor where only the day before Mrs. Harvey had entertained ladies for tea. Tables were overturned; lamps and precious gewgaws were shattered—you'd have thought a typhoon had passed through. But it was on the silk-brocaded chaise that poor Floyd beheld the most awful sight of all, a sight that would have stopped any but the stoutest heart, the strangled, lifeless body of—"

"Mr. Harvey!" I said.

Mr. Stone closed his mouth and narrowed his eyes. "No, smarty-pants, *not* Mr. Harvey. *Mrs.* Harvey."

"But you *said*—" I started to argue.

"I am not done yet," said Mr. Stone. "Here."

He held out the bag of marshmallows to me. "Stick a couple in your mouth and keep them there. Now," he went on, "where was I? Oh, yes—and this is one of the queer parts—that big black cat was curled up in her lap, and later Floyd told people it was as though the cat was trying to bring back the warmth to his mistress's cold, dead body."

When Mr. Stone paused to sip his hot chocolate, neither Yasmeen nor I said a word. We were too caught up in the spookiness.

"Two days later," Mr. Stone continued, "Marianne Harvey was buried—right here at St. Bernard's, by the way, the marker is there for all to see—and her grieving husband wept at the graveside. Mr. Harvey told the police he had been unexpectedly called over the mountain to Belleburg the morning of the murder. While he was gone, he said, some thief must have broken in and surprised his wife.

"Well, the thief was never caught. In fact, no one ever saw hide nor hair of any thief. Add to that the fact that Mr. Harvey was not a popular man, and you can infer the rumors that flew.

Some people speculated that Marianne Harvey was miserable in her marriage, that her husband had mistreated her, that she had had a sweetheart and when Mr. Harvey found out, he killed her in a jealous rage. Some speculated that it was poor stouthearted Floyd himself who was the sweetheart. But if there was evidence one way or the other, I never heard about it. And in those days no one had the guts to stand up to the richest man in town.

"A few days passed, and the weather grew colder. Finally, it was Halloween night. Wisps of cloud obscured the full moon. A gentleman walking home from a local tavern passed the Harvey house and heard a ruckus inside. Now, this gentleman had been at the tavern for some hours, and so not everyone credited his account with perfect accuracy. What he claimed he heard were three sounds at once—a mountain lion's scream, the howl of a madman, and the rough-and-tumble of a barroom brawl. This cater-wumpus lasted perhaps one minute. And then there was an eerie silence.

"Not being so stouthearted as Floyd, the fellow hightailed it to the courthouse, which in those days was also the headquarters for the police. And so it was an officer of the law who opened the parlor door at the Harvey house on Halloween night and found the mangled corpse of . . ."

Yasmeen said, "Mr. Harvey."

Mr. Stone nodded. "It was a grisly scene. Mr. Harvey had locked up the parlor after his wife died there, but he or someone else had opened it up that night. There was blood everywhere—streaking the rugs and the walls, splattered on the ceiling. And the body"—Mr. Stone shuddered as if he had seen it himself, which I guess he had in his imagination—"it was unrecognizable, just as though some beast of the jungle had wrought revenge."

"Where was the cat?" Yasmeen asked.

Mr. Stone nodded. "Well you might ask," he said. "There had been a fire in the fireplace, and a few hot embers remained. The cat was on the hearth, absorbing the last of the warmth and cleaning something red and sticky from its paws."

Chapter Seventeen

"Ewwww!" Yasmeen and I said.

Mr. Stone smiled and folded his hands in front of him on the table. He looked pleased with himself. "That's the story, just as my dad told it. I'm surprised I still remember."

"But what about the ghost?" I asked.

Mr. Stone got up from the table and cleared our cups. "Ah yes, the ghost," he said. "It seems that old man Harvey's ghost still haunts the mansion he built for himself and his bride, and those who have lived there since have spent many a sleepless night."

"I've heard cats in College Springs often get catnapped around Halloween," I said. "And sometimes whoever it is blames the ghost. This year there are five missing cats already."

"Really?" said Mr. Stone. "That's a shame. It would seem the Harvey ghost is not entirely rational. Having been killed by his wife's cat, he seeks revenge on *all* cats."

Yasmeen looked disgusted. "You don't really believe in ghosts, do you, Mr. Stone?"

"The older I get, the more I find the world to be mysterious," Mr. Stone said.

"In the story, what happened to the poor cat? Marianne Harvey's cat?" I asked.

"The 'poor cat'?" Mr. Stone said. "The 'poor cat' was a bloodthirsty killer!"

"But it doesn't sound like his victim, Mr. Harvey, was a very nice man," Yasmeen said.

"*Or* a very nice ghost," I said.

"We don't know for certain what kind of man Mr. Harvey was," Mr. Stone said.

Yasmeen disagreed. "The cat knew," she said.

I looked at Yasmeen. "It seems kind of

strange that you're totally ready to accept a cat witnessing a murder and getting revenge, but you're totally rejecting the idea of ghosts."

"What's so strange about it?" Yasmeen said. "I don't believe in ghosts. I do believe in cats."

Mr. Stone didn't give me time to puzzle that one out. "As the story goes," he said, "Marianne Harvey's cat suffered the sorry fate that is common to unwanted felines—he was put in a sack with a great number of rocks and thrown into a pool of water, in this case the Harveys' well. People said his howling was enough to freeze your blood."

Yasmeen and I both felt better when we left Mr. Stone's house. It couldn't have been the gory ghost story that cheered us up. It must have been the hot chocolate and marshmallows.

"Let's go back to St. Bernard's," I suggested, "to see where Marianne Harvey is buried."

"I can't," Yasmeen said. "I'm going over to see the Lees' new baby. My whole family has to. But—I know, Alex—why don't you go over to the cemetery? Maybe what's going on *is* a Halloween prank, and somebody's eventually going to blame the whole thing on the ghost. You might notice something new at the cemetery."

This time it was me who opened my mouth and closed it again. I never thought of going to the cemetery *alone*. But Yasmeen already had plenty of reasons to call me a wimp. If I refused to go, she'd have plenty plus one.

"No problem," I said, trying to sound like I meant it. "I'll call you after dinner." Then I turned around and started walking toward St. Bernard's, all the time thinking, "Provided the ghosts don't get me first."

Chapter Eighteen

The last time I had paid a visit to my local grave-yard, my cat had paused to do a little personal grooming beside a statue of a grumpy angel. As it turned out, that angel was Marianne Harvey's grave marker.

Actually, the angel was pretty close to the gate, but that day I turned right when I walked in, and I wound around searching among a lot of other headstones before I came to it. By the time I did, the light was almost gone, and I had to stare to read the inscription:

MARIANNE MCCLELLAN HARVEY
BORN JULY 2, 1854
DIED OCTOBER 28, 1879
IN DEATH, THE ETERNAL WIFE.

It was dark and cold. I was in a cemetery. The leafless trees looked sharp and thorny against the rising moon. Can you blame me for feeling creeped out?

And that inscription didn't help. It was like it condemned poor Marianne to be stuck with her murderous husband forever.

Mr. Stone had said Mr. Harvey was buried next to Marianne, but searching still took me a few minutes. In the end, I had to brush away dirt to read the inscription. When I did, it was even stranger than his wife's.

GILMORE SAMUEL HARVEY
BORN DECEMBER 2, 1836
DIED OCTOBER 31, 1879
SO SHALL THE RIGHTEOUS
ESCAPE THE GRAVE.

Now not only was I creeped out, I had something to think about. Maybe this was crazy, but it almost felt like that one was trying to tell me something. But what?

A cold gust made me shiver, and I noticed the bats were out again. If there was ever a moment for ghosts and vampires and werewolves to appear in a regular kid's life, this was it.

I started to run. I didn't get very far.

That night after dinner I called Yasmeen to fill her in. I swear, even over the phone line, I could hear her shake her head, exasperated. "That's why I carry Band-Aids and antiseptic," she said.

I touched my forehead to see if it still hurt. It did. I think it was Dad's scrubbing that inflicted most of the damage, but it hadn't been such a hot idea to run into the tree in the first place.

"Anybody would've been scared," I said. "Anybody would've run."

"Anybody would not have run into a *tree*," she said. "It takes the distinctive talents of my next-door neighbor Alex Parakeet to do that."

"Can we change the subject?" I said.

"Absolutely," Yasmeen said. "The new subject is how you're going to help me do Mrs. Lee a favor."

"That wasn't the new subject I was thinking of," I said, "but what favor?"

"We're supposed to return one of the baby monitors—the fancy one from Mrs. Jensen. Marjie Lee says it's too powerful. She keeps picking up cell phone conversations, and it's embarrassing."

"But why are *you* doing this?" I asked her.

"*We* are doing this because my mom volunteered us," Yasmeen said. "Come on, Alex. It's only over to Biggest Buy-Buy. We can walk there after school."

There was no way carrying one baby monitor required two people. But there was also no way I was going to get out of this if Yasmeen had made up her mind. So I said, "Sure. Now can we talk about my subject?"

"Sure," Yasmeen said.

"I told you about the gravestones, what they said?"

"Right," said Yasmeen.

"Well, didn't it seem strange to you—especially Mr. Harvey's?"

"It's unusual," she agreed, "but every Christian believes Jesus rose from the grave so that we will, too. Isn't that all he was saying?"

Something hit me. "Wait a second. Isn't that all *who* was saying?"

"Who else are we talking about?" Yasmeen said. "Gilmore Harvey."

"Gilmore Harvey wrote what it said on Marianne's headstone. He was there to do it after she died. But *when* did he write his own?" I asked. "He died all of a sudden. It's not like he had time to be composing his own—what do you call it? An epo—?"

"An epitaph," Yasmeen said slowly, like she was thinking as she spoke. "So unless he had it ready to go in advance, he didn't write it. Someone else did."

"Someone else," I repeated, "but who?"

"I don't know," she said, still like she was thinking. But then her voice changed. "Look,

Alex, this is all ancient history, right? It's not helping us find the missing cats."

"You sent me to the cemetery!" I protested.

"That was because I thought you might find a clue to what's going on in this century—the twenty-first century, not the nineteenth. I think we better forget about the cemetery for now. Don't you want to hear about the baby? And Mr. Lee was even there."

"Amazing."

"That's what my mom said. You know what's kind of a weird coincidence? The baby's room is all decorated with pictures of cats—big ones like lions and cheetahs and lynxes. Mrs. Lee told us it's because of Mr. Lee's business."

"What is his business anyway?" I asked. "All I know is that nobody ever sees him."

"His business is exotic pets," Yasmeen said. "He travels all over the world buying and selling. His customers are super-rich people who want something unusual."

"Pets?" I said. "Yasmeen, what if . . . ?"

"What if what?"

"What if Mr. Lee has something to do with the missing cats?"

"You aren't listening, Alex. No offense to Luau, but there is nothing exotic about a house cat."

"Not here in Pennsylvania," I said, "but maybe somewhere house cats are exotic, or— what about this? What if he *does* something to them to make them exotic?"

There was a pause, and I could hear Yasmeen breathing. Then she said, "No. No way. If you ever got a chance to talk to Mr. Lee, you'd see. He's nice, really."

My head hurt. And arguing with Yasmeen would only make it worse. So I didn't. But all the same, this is what I was thinking: Was Mr. Lee really the nice guy she thought he was? Or could he be a serial catnapper?

Chapter Nineteen

Mom walked into the family room as I was hanging up the phone. She was just getting home and still had her uniform on. She tried to smile at me and say, "Hi, honey," but she was yawning, so her face got twisted and her words came out, "Hi-yuh-ee." Then she took a good look and woke right up. "What on earth happened to your *head*?" she asked.

I touched the bandage. "Little accident. I'm okay."

"Did your dad clean it up?" she asked.

"*Oh*, yeah," I said. "I think he used steel wool."

Mom looked sad. "I wish I had been home to do it, but somebody's got to make College Springs safe for decent people—and decent cats."

"Anything new?" I asked.

"Another cat is missing," Mom said.

"Another negligent owner?" I asked.

Mom dropped into the big, comfy chair, closed her eyes, and nodded. "I may never figure this one out, but at least you got a new vocabulary word."

"And did this one see the thief in action?"

"Saw something, but no good description," Mom said. "I swear, whoever this is moves like a ghost."

My ears pricked up. "A ghost?" I said. "See, Mom. Maybe it really is—"

Mom silenced me with a look. Obviously, she did not want to hear any more from me about ghosts. Should I tell her my suspicion about Mr. Lee? But I didn't think she'd appreciate me suspecting our next-door neighbor without an atom of evidence either. So I asked a different question. "Did you have a chance to talk to Kyle's family?"

"For quite a while," she said. "They were a positive joy after the other folks I've been visiting lately. Except that boy is morbid, don't you think? I asked what he does for fun, and he said, 'I visit the cemetery across the street.' "

"Did you notice anything else about Kyle?" I asked Mom. "Like was he—I dunno—*scared* of you or anything?"

I was thinking of how nervous he had seemed in the cafeteria when he told Yasmeen and me to stop detecting. If it scared him for *us* to investigate Halloween's disappearance, wouldn't he be terrified by a police detective asking questions?

"He did seem anxious," Mom said. "But it fit in with him being an odd kind of kid. What did Fred call him? A Gloomy Gus?"

"What else did you find out?" I asked.

"That Fred Krichels was right about something else," Mom said, "that little sister of his—Cammie. I think I am now a leading authority on the life of Cammie. She's making a unicorn out of play dough at preschool. Her favorite song is 'The Cat Came Back.' " Mom shook her head and laughed. "Yah-yak-yak—gosh, a kid like that can get on your nerves!"

Shoot, I thought. Was my mom as bad as Officer Krichels? People who are little and annoying are not necessarily dumb, too. Mom pulled her notebook out of her back pocket and flipped through the pages.

"Here it is," Mom said. "According to Cammie, Kyle *tortured* the poor cat." She read from the notebook: " 'He always went around yanking Halloween's ears and pouring poison in them.' "

"What?" I tried to picture pale, sad-faced Kyle hurting a fly, let alone his own cat.

Mom laughed, which wasn't precisely what I expected when she had just told me about a kid torturing a cat. "Alex," she said, "haven't you ever yanked on Luau's ears and poured poison in them?"

I was shocked. "Of course not. Luau's my buddy!"

"Oh yes?" She was still smiling. "Let me ask you something else. Do the words *ear mites* ring a bell?"

Ohhhh. Now I got it. Ear mites are tiny, itchy bugs. If your cat gets them, it goes crazy trying to scratch, so the vet gives you a bottle of eardrops. When I gave them to Luau, he hated it—kept trying to wriggle away while I held tight.

"Cammie must have seen Kyle treating the ear mites and thought he was torturing his cat," I said.

Mom nodded. "Plus she's a typical kid, loved tattling on her big brother. I double-checked with his parents. They even showed me the bottle from the vet."

Good old Mom. She had solved one mystery, at least. Kyle did love his cat. You would never go to the trouble of "yanking its ears and pouring poison in them" if you didn't.

Chapter Twenty

The next day turned out to be one of those unusual ones where everything we did in school actually required the use of my brain. That meant I didn't have a chance to think about who stole Halloween—not to mention five other cats—till Yasmeen and I were on our way home.

As we turned the corner onto Chickadee Court my stomach rumbled. Dad hadn't made it to the grocery store yesterday, so instead of a sandwich there was a Ziploc bag of Pirate Berry Crunch in my lunch. And Pirate Berry Crunch just doesn't stick with you.

Thinking of soup, I said, "What if we talk to Bub again?"

Yasmeen was hungry, too. "Good idea."

Bub had another guest in his living room when we walked in. This one was curled up on the recliner with his head resting on the remote. On TV was a black-and-white movie with the sound turned down. In it a pretty lady on scaffolding was trying to fix a big dinosaur skeleton.

Bub nodded at the set. *"Bringing Up Baby,"* he said. " 'Baby' is a leopard—and from the feline point of view, a dish. Luau purrs every time she comes on."

Luau heard his name, stretched, and rolled over, exposing his tummy. I tickled him, and he *mrrrrow*ed and batted at my hand, which meant, *Please, Alex, not in front of the neighbors!*

Bub served us lentil soup and sat down at the head of the table. "How's the other guy look?" he asked me.

It took me a second to realize he was talking about the Band-Aid on my forehead. "The other guy was a tree," I said.

Bub nodded thoughtfully. "There's been a lotta that lately," he said, "trees attacking innocent kids. I saw it on Fox."

Bub tried to keep his face straight but couldn't. He laughed and laughed, which made me laugh, too. Yasmeen shook her head like we were a couple of kindergartners. Finally Bub wiped the tears from his face with a paper towel and asked us how the case was going.

"We're kind of at a dead end," Yasmeen said. Then she told him about the missing cats with their negligent owners and about Halloween's ear mites. She did not tell him about Mr. Lee, I noticed. She still thought I was crazy to suspect he might be stealing cats for his exotic pet business.

"Still no sign of a ransom note, though?" Bub said.

"Mom said Kyle seemed anxious," I told him. "But he didn't say anything about a ransom note. And I guess none of the other cat owners did either."

Yasmeen and I were finishing our soup when we heard the doorbell ring. Officer Krichels? Al, the delivery man? It could even have been Dad. "Come on in, it's open!" Bub called, and into Bub's house walked the last person we wanted to see, Sophie Sikora.

I looked at Yasmeen, who looked at me, and our identical expressions said, *Oh, no.*

On her way in, Sophie bumped the recliner, which made Luau *mrrrrrow.* When she got to where we were sitting at the table, she ran into that, too. It's a good thing our bowls were almost empty, or there would have been a couple of soup tsunamis right into our laps.

"Hey, Bub!" Sophie greeted us. "Hey, Yazzie and Al! What's the haps?"

Nobody calls me "Al." And my dad is the only person allowed to call Yasmeen "Yazzie." We both opened our mouths to set Sophie straight, but she kept right on talking. "*I* just fixed Billy's remote control jeep," she said. "Mrs. Jensen paid me, too. It was a whole *lot* she paid me, but I can't tell you how much, because you'd be *so* jealous, and my mom says I shouldn't brag, even though my dad says it's okay provided you have something to brag *about*, like I do, because I'm so good at fixing stuff, so how much she paid me was ten dollars."

Bub set a bowl of soup in front of her, and she started shoveling. For a moment I understood what my mom means when she talks about "blessed silence." But soon she slurped the last of her soup and started in again.

"Did you notice how Bub's doorbell worked so good when I rang it?" she said. "I'm the one that fixed it. Bub didn't pay me though, but I'm not saying I care, because some people don't have money like the Jensens do. My family has a lot of money because my dad earns thousands and thousands every year—I forget how many thousands—only my mom says the Jensens have an ungodly amount of money. *Ungodly* is a word that means 'even more than us.' My mom also says—"

"Sophie?" Bub's expression was patient.

"Yes, Bub?"

"Sometimes the things mom says are best left with mom."

It took a second for that to sink in. Then

Sophie said, "You mean I should shut the heck up?"

Bub nodded.

Sophie shrugged. "Okay."

I got up and took Yasmeen's and my bowls to the kitchen. When I came back to the table, Bub was twiddling his thumbs, a sure sign he was thinking.

"Have you got an idea about the case?" I asked him.

He nodded. "Ah, yup. But I don't know what good it's gonna do you. Think a bit—except for Kyle's, what do the missing cats have in common?"

"The owners were negligent," Yasmeen said.

Bub nodded. "So it seems like your thief is particularly after cats that aren't well taken care of. Now, why would that be?"

Of course I knew about the coincidence. But I hadn't thought much about what it might mean. And there was the problem that Kyle's cat Halloween didn't fit the pattern. Maybe because Halloween was stolen by a different thief? But then I thought of something else. "Kyle's little sister didn't think *he* was taking good care of Halloween either!" I said. "Maybe she told other people, and—"

Bub nodded. "She was happy enough to tell the police."

"So," Yasmeen said, "it might be that the thief isn't really *stealing* cats. Maybe he's *rescuing* cats. Maybe he's a good guy, not a bad guy."

"I don't know about that," Bub said. "Stealing is stealing even if your motives are good. Think what would happen if everybody took it into their heads to 'rescue' other folks' possessions."

My mom would have to work even more overtime, I thought, and I was about to say so, but the phone rang and Bub got up from the table to answer it.

It is funny how sometimes one thing leads to another. Later, we found out it was Jo, Bub's niece, on the phone. Jo is a student at the university. The dryer in her dorm was broken. She called to ask if she could use Bub's.

If the dorm dryer hadn't broken, Jo wouldn't

have called. If Jo hadn't called, Bub never would have left us alone when he did.

And if Bub hadn't left us alone, Yasmeen would have told *him* her idea, and he would have said it was too risky, and we would have forgotten about it.

So in a way, everything that happened next was because the dryer in Jo's dorm at the university broke down two days before Halloween.

Chapter Twenty-one

Yasmeen's crazy idea was this: Spread the word that Luau was a neglected cat, too, a cat that badly needed rescuing. College Springs is a dinky town. If we told enough people, pretty soon the thief would hear about it—same as he must have heard about Kyle "torturing" Halloween. When that happened, the thief would go after Luau.

"And that's when we get him!" Yasmeen said.

There was a pause, and during the pause I expected her to say, "Ha-ha."

Only she didn't.

So finally I had to say, *"What?"*

And Sophie said, "Wow, Yasmeen. I never saw before why people said you were smart, but now I finally see because that is just *so smart*—"

"Hey—aren't your lips supposed to be zipped?" I said.

"Don't be rude, Alex," Yasmeen said. "Thank you, Sophie."

"Oh, that's great, now you're ganging up on me, not to mention poor, innocent Luau. . . ."

My cat had been peacefully watching the glamorous leopard on TV, but now his ears perked up and he said, *"mrrrrf,"* which meant, *Did I hear my name mentioned?*

"I admit the plan still has some bugs that need working out . . . ," Yasmeen said.

"No, it doesn't," I said. "No bugs because no plan. Not gonna happen."

"Listen a minute," said Yasmeen.

"No."

"Seriously."

"No."

"We could fix it so Luau isn't in any danger," she said. "We could be *really* careful."

I crossed my arms over my chest and shook my head. Luau, meanwhile, jumped off the recliner and walked toward us. I expected him to hide under my chair—seeking protection from the crazy person with the crazy plan—but Luau, that traitor, jumped into Yasmeen's lap instead.

"See?" she said. "He's volunteering."

"You get down from there!" I said.

Sophie interrupted. "I could keep him safe if I had the right equipment. I could 'wire' him like the FBI does. You know, hide a radio transmitter on his body so we could hear whatever was happening to him—"

"That is totally insane," I protested. "I mean, apart from everything else, don't you geniuses see the obvious problem? People wear clothes. Cats don't. Where are you going to hide a transmitter?"

"A collar would be enough," Sophie said. "If the transmitter is small, it could dangle from it. Are there stores for teensy transmitters? I bet

I could take something apart. Like a wireless phone? Or a walkie-talkie? It has to use radio waves—"

As soon as Sophie said it, I remembered Yasmeen already had precisely the right source for such a transmitter. It was at her house, waiting to go back to Biggest Buy-Buy. Would Yasmeen remember it, too? I tried mental telepathy: Forget, forget, forget. . . .

It didn't work.

"The baby monitor!" Yasmeen said. "Mrs. Lee says it's *too* powerful! Plus it's really small. I've got it at home. Instead of returning it, we can sort of, you know, *borrow* it."

"*Steal* it, you mean," I said.

"We'll return it later—"

"After Sophie takes it apart?" I said.

Yasmeen shrugged. "We are not talking about Humpty-Dumpty, Alex. We are talking about simple electronics. After she takes it apart, she'll put it back together."

I never officially changed my mind and agreed to go along with this nutso plan. But at some point it became unavoidable, like a thunderstorm when the clouds bunch up. And when Bub came back from talking to Jo, I didn't tell him what was going on. Instead, the three of us—Yasmeen, Sophie, and I—looked at each other and it instantly became a kids-against-the-grown-ups alliance. I have noticed that this happens sometimes—usually when kids are about to do something totally clever that they know is also totally stupid.

Later, we finalized our plans. Sophie is the most spoiled kid on Chickadee Court, which for once was coming in handy. She was pretty sure her mom would buy her the collar if she said it was for one of her millions of stuffed animals. Meanwhile, Yasmeen would bring the baby monitor to Sophie's right away so she could work on modifying it for its new purpose. The big problem was that the transmitter's signal would need to be amplified. Sophie had an idea for doing this, but she wasn't sure it would work.

"There's one more job," Yasmeen told Sophie. "And it's important. You have to tell everybody how badly Alex treats Luau."

"But everybody knows about Luau and me," I said. "Who would believe I treat him bad?"

"*Badly,*" Yasmeen said. "And we've been over this. There's only one person who has to believe it, and that's the catnapper. We just start the rumor and wait. I know who I'm calling—Billy Jensen."

I didn't say anything to my parents about the plan. I wasn't sure it was going to happen, for one thing. Telling them could wait. But there was someone I needed to consult right away. At bedtime he was sitting on my pillow with his favorite possession, the white ball of catnip.

"Was Yasmeen right today, Luau?" I asked him. "Were you volunteering when you jumped into her lap? You know it could be dangerous. You could end up catnapped yourself."

Luau slithered beneath my sheet and blanket, purring. It took me a minute to understand, but when I did, I had to laugh.

"Luau Kitty," I said, "goes *undercover.*"

Chapter Twenty-two

I could have told you about seventy-five reasons this plan of Yasmeen's was bad. But there was one I never thought of—its effect on *me*. Billy Jensen was totally true to his reputation as the biggest blabbermouth in first grade, if not the entire school. He wasted no time spreading the rumor about how I mistreat Luau.

And Yasmeen hadn't left it at plain old "mistreat" either. She provided *details*. Supposedly, I buy Luau dog food instead of cat food because it's cheaper, and I make him sleep in the garage no matter how freezing it gets.

The next day, Thursday, it seemed like half the school wasn't talking to me. I even caught Mrs. Timmons glaring at me once, at the same time she brushed a few white cat hairs off her shoulder. One girl, a second-grader, hissed and clawed the air when she passed me in the hall.

"I'm really sorry, but it won't be for long," Yasmeen told me at lunch. We were the only ones at the table because no one else wanted to sit with me. "And for now, you should be glad it's going so well."

"I hope Sophie works fast," I said.

"I talked to Sophie this morning after recess," Yasmeen said. "She pitched one of her famous fits, and her mom went straight to the pet store for a cat collar. Sophie says those fits never fail. She thinks she can do the work today after school. The monitor should be ready by Halloween—tomorrow."

I swallowed the last bite of my peanut butter sandwich and gulped some milk. "I think we should go over the plan again," I said. "I'm not sure I've got it totally straight."

Yasmeen nodded. "The catnapper usually strikes around midnight. So tomorrow after trick-or-treating, you'll put Luau's new collar on him and let him out."

"Right," I said.

"You've got the cat bed ready, right?"

"I can put it on the front step. For the catnapper it'll be like an invitation," I said.

"Good," Yasmeen said. "But just in case there's a problem, you'll have the baby monitor, the receiver half."

"But that's only for emergencies," I said.

"If everything goes the way I think it will," Yasmeen said, "we won't even have to use it."

"So Luau's safely in his bed . . . ," I said, "and then comes the hard part."

Yasmeen nodded. "You *have to* stay awake until 3 A.M., watching out the window—making sure Luau's okay. Then, assuming he is, I take over. You'll know it's okay to go to sleep when I blink the lights in my bedroom. That means I'm on duty."

"And if Luau's not still safe—if I see somebody in the yard . . . ?"

"Shine a light!" Yasmeen said, just the way she would in church.

I laughed. "And what do you think will happen then," I asked, "when I *shine a light*?"

"I *think* whoever it is will drop Luau and run, but by then we will have seen him."

"Or her," I said.

Yasmeen nodded. "And anyway, if he or she doesn't drop Luau, we've got the transmitter in the collar. What we hear will tell us where Luau is, and we'll rescue him."

When I got home from school, my dad was in the kitchen making dinner. Usually a gourmet dinner by Dad means using stuff out of two cardboard boxes instead of one, but now he was looking at an actual cookbook.

"Check it out." Dad pointed a wooden spoon at a pan on the stove. "Plus—look at this: *Fresh* vegetables."

I looked over his shoulder and saw two onions and some broccoli. Yuck.

"I'm making stir-fry," Dad said. "I borrowed the cookbook from Marjie Lee." He measured a spoonful of soy sauce into a bowl and frowned. "Doesn't seem like very much."

I looked at the recipe. "It says one quarter *cup*, Dad."

Dad said, "I knew that."

"So I guess the pills aren't helping your eyes any," I said.

"In fact, I think my vision's better," Dad said. "But this print is so darned small, isn't it? Which reminds me, Alex—sometime before dinner, would you run over to Mr. Blanco's store and pick up the rest of my pills?"

I said sure, thinking I hadn't had a chance to ask Mr. Blanco what he knew about the ghost story. Dad rinsed the broccoli and began cutting it up.

"How come you borrowed a cookbook?" I asked him.

"I noticed it on the shelf when I went over to see the baby. Marjie said go ahead and take it. I've been thinking I should get more serious about cooking—especially vegetables. They're good for eyesight, too, you know."

I got a handful of cookies out of the cupboard and sat down to eat them at the kitchen table. If Dad was going to get serious about vegetables, I'd better fortify myself. "What's the baby like?" I asked him.

"Scrunched-up face on one end, diaper on the other," Dad said. "It's a while before they get cute."

"What did they name her?"

Dad smiled. "Marjie Lee can't decide, which is *so* like her. For now, they're calling her Boopsie."

"That's awful!" I said. "Doesn't Mr. Lee have an idea what to name her?"

"Who knows?" Dad said. "The man is practically a ghost—nobody ever sees him. You just hear tell he's been around."

My ears pricked up. Mr. Lee was like a ghost? Maybe he really *was* the catnapper!

But I didn't want to say that. Mr. Lee was a neighbor, and my reasons for suspecting him were lame. Reason one: He was in a business that had to do with animals, and cats are missing, and cats are animals. Reason two: He is never around, which makes him seem mysterious, and the thief is also mysterious.

There was something more as well, though. I didn't know what to call it. *Instinct* maybe? My instinct told me not to trust Mr. Lee.

I tried to be subtle. "You didn't notice anything unusual at the Lees' house when you were there, did you, Dad? Like new *pets* maybe?"

"Isn't a new baby enough?" Dad said.

I tried again. "So, uh, what do you know about Mr. Lee? I mean, what kind of a guy is he? What about his business?"

Dad looked over his shoulder at me. "Why this sudden neighborly interest, Alex?"

I swallowed the last bite of cookie. "I don't know," I lied. "Just curiosity is all."

Dad squinted at the recipe again. Then he measured a spoonful of oil and poured it into the pan. "Well, Alex," he said. "You know what they say. 'Twas curiosity that killed the cat."

Chapter Twenty-three

The day had started out sunny, but by now a silver sheet of clouds had drifted in, and the air felt cold. To keep warm, I ran partway to Mr. Blanco's store at the Harvey house. Walking up the path, I noticed most of the pumpkins were gone from the front yard. Inside, the lights were bright. The store seemed to be open, but there was no one around.

"Hello? Mr. Blanco?" I called.

"Hello!" came a voice. "Who's there?"

I still didn't see anyone, and I couldn't figure out where the voice was coming from. Knowing this was the Harvey house—the famous *haunted* Harvey house—I felt a little weird conversing with a voice that didn't have a body.

"It's me, Alex Parakeet! Is that you, Mr. Blanco?"

"I think so," the voice said, "but I'm so covered with dust and cobwebs I can't be sure. Hang on. I'll be up in a minute."

Oh, that's right. Mom had mentioned that there was a cellar. That's where the neighbors found the starving cats that time. Sure enough, a moment later Mr. Blanco emerged from a doorway in a back corner. With one hand he was carrying a big black book—about twice the size of a photo album—and some old yellow newspapers. With the other hand he was wiping cobwebs from his face. I hoped no spiders had hitched a ride in his hair.

"Did you come for the rest of the pills?" he asked. "I've got a new batch up by the register. And maybe you'd like some ointment for that bruise on your forehead? It looks painful."

"It doesn't hurt anymore," I said, "but thanks."

"How are the pills working out for your dad?" Mr. Blanco asked.

I followed him to the front of the store. He dropped the book and the newspapers onto the counter. They landed with a bump and a poof of dust.

"Dad thinks they're helping," I said, "but I'm not sure."

"They're made in small batches," Mr. Blanco said, "which is why your dad had to wait for these." He pulled the yellow bottle of pills from underneath the counter. "Anything else I can get you?"

I looked around and noticed the white balls I had seen last time, the ones that looked like the catnip sachet we found under the car. *Shoot!* I had meant to ask about them then, but when the ghost howled and turned out the lights, I totally forgot.

"Are these catnip?" I asked.

Mr. Blanco nodded. "One of my most popular sellers. Cat owners are crazy people—have you noticed? Oh—sorry, Alex. Present company excepted."

"I guess you wouldn't remember any particular person who bought one of these catnip things?"

"Do you have somebody in mind?" Mr. Blanco asked.

I wanted to say, yeah—I have in mind your basic catnapper. Do you have any catnapper customers? But instead, I explained that Yasmeen and I had found one on Groundhog Drive by St. Bernard's.

"You wanted to return it to the rightful owner, is that it?" Mr. Blanco said. "Well, in that neighborhood, I'd say it was probably Kyle Richmond. Talk about your crazy cat-owners." Mr. Blanco shook his head.

"Kyle?" I felt crushed. If the catnip was Kyle's, it wasn't a clue at all.

"Come to think of it," Mr. Blanco said, "he's another kid that's seen the ghost, same as you and Yasmeen. He was in Sunday afternoon to buy catnip and started asking questions about the ghost story."

"Mr. Stone told Yasmeen and me his dad's

version of the story," I said. "I even went over to the cemetery to see the grave markers. I was hoping you might know more."

"That's one reason I've been digging around this house," Mr. Blanco said, "to find out what really happened. Living across from the cemetery, Kyle's interested in ghosts, too. Anyway, we were talking when the usual ruckus kicked up. He was outta here before the lights blinked. Poor kid—he hasn't been back."

I said that was too bad, then I asked about the stuff Mr. Blanco had brought up from the cellar. "Does this have to do with the ghost story?"

He pushed the book and the newspapers toward me. "They're from around the time the murders took place," he said. "And yesterday I found something strange, too. We're still remodeling, you know, and I punched through a wall in the room I think must have been the parlor."

"That's where Mr. Stone told us the bodies were found," I said, "Marianne Harvey's first, and then, on Halloween night, her husband's."

Mr. Blanco nodded. "Well, punching through that wall, darned if I didn't find an old fireplace. And it must've been covered over in a hurry, too, because there were still traces of burned junk there."

"Junk?" I said. "Like somebody burned trash in the fireplace?"

Mr. Blanco shrugged. "I wouldn't have thought so—not in an upscale house like this. Let me show you." He pulled a plastic bag out of a drawer, then laid it on the counter beside the papers and the book. The bag's contents were black and dusty, but after a minute I realized they were burned fragments of cloth—someone's clothes maybe.

"Can I open the bag?" I said.

"Not in here, if you don't mind," Mr. Blanco said. "It makes a heck of a mess. You probably think I'm crazy saving it at all, huh?"

"No, I don't," I said. "Ever since Yasmeen dragged me into that mystery last Christmas, I understand how detecting takes over your brain."

Mr. Blanco agreed. "The more I find, the more I wonder. For example, I grant it's a good story, but does it really seem likely that a house cat could kill a human being?"

Mr. Blanco kept talking, but I didn't hear what he said. Was I imagining it? Or did I feel a gust of cold air?

"And then there's this stuff here," Mr. Blanco was saying. "Who would have been burning clothes in the fireplace, and why?"

I tried to ignore the goose bumps prickling my arms. "But how do you know the burned clothes have anything to do with the murders?" I asked. "Haven't a lot of people lived in this house?"

"Quite a few," he said. "But the clothes almost have to come from around the same time. I have some old photos of the house, and that fireplace has been walled up since before the turn of the twentieth century."

I was going to ask him what other stuff he had found, but an unearthly howl interrupted me—like a giant-size cat with its tail pinched under a rocking chair. I looked at Mr. Blanco expecting to see fear in his face, but he only sighed and shook his head. "Here we go again."

Chapter Twenty-four

The howl, the lightning, the crack of thunder, and finally the lights blacking out. The ghost had paid another visit to the Harvey House Health Boutique, but it wasn't so scary this time, I guess because I kind of knew what to expect. It seems like a lot of what's scary in the world is the possibility of the *un*expected. Anyway, now I thought the ghostly activity was more like a signal than a treat.

But a signal for what?

After Mr. Blanco turned the lights back on, he gave me one of the catnip balls for Luau "because you're a good customer," and he let me borrow the dusty newspapers and the big black book. "I won't have time to look at them tonight, anyway," he said. "You being an experienced detective and all, maybe you'll figure out what really happened."

Fat chance, I thought. I can't even solve the case of a cat stolen last week—how could I expect to figure out anything new about murders from the nineteenth century?

At home, Dad thanked me for the pills and Luau thanked me for the catnip. Then I went over to Yasmeen's to report the latest and ask for her help.

"What's that dusty old junk?" Yasmeen wanted to know when I dropped the book and the newspapers on the coffee table in her family room.

I told her Mr. Blanco had found them. "Now he wants me to look through them and help figure out the truth about the ghost," I explained, "but I need your superior brainpower."

Yasmeen loves to be told how superior her brainpower is, so she said sure—even though she doesn't believe in ghosts.

Then I told her the bad news about the catnip we found, that it was probably Kyle's.

Yasmeen sighed and shook her head. "So our one and only clue isn't?"

Brains are peculiar things. I guess because we were talking about clues, mine suddenly filled up with that dream from a few days ago, the one where all the clues turned into fish and swam away—all except one slip of paper.

"Yasmeen," I said, "what did you do with the other clues?"

"Aren't you listening?" she asked. "We don't *have* any other clues."

"I mean the other stuff we found when we found the catnip," I said.

"Oh—the beer can and junk," she said. "In my room. I didn't think we should throw anything out till we were done with our detecting."

"Let's take another look," I said. "We can check out Mr. Blanco's stuff later. The ghost has been around for more than one hundred years—he isn't going anywhere."

Upstairs, Yasmeen retrieved the bag from a

shelf. "Besides the can, there's a gum wrapper and some kind of receipt."

"That was it." I took the bag from her. "A grocery receipt."

We looked at each other.

"A grocery receipt!" Yasmeen conked her head with her fist. "We must be the *stupidest* smart kids yet!"

The receipt was from the Smartt Mart on Northernmost Parkway. Unfortunately, it didn't have a credit card number or a name. But there was a list of what had been purchased and the date, October 22, the same day Halloween disappeared.

"What kind of recipe uses ten boxes of salt and twenty pounds of flour?" I asked Yasmeen.

"I don't know." Yasmeen made a face. "But I wouldn't want to eat it."

"Besides that, there're five packages of food coloring—"

"Assorted colors," Yasmeen cut in. She was looking over my shoulder.

"*And* ten twenty-pound bags of cat food."

Yasmeen moaned. "We've had this for four days, and we never even looked at it."

"Yup, we're idiots, all right," I said. "We were totally focused on catnip, and this was right in front of our faces."

Looking at the receipt, Yasmeen asked, "Is that a good brand of cat food?"

"The kind the vet likes." I nodded.

"So it looks like we're right about that, at least," Yasmeen said. "The catnapper *likes* cats; he probably sees himself as a cat rescue squad."

I went back to studying the receipt. Flour, salt, and food coloring. What could a person do with that? I knew some animals—like cows and horses—need extra salt, but I never heard of cats needing it. And anyway, it didn't explain the flour or the food coloring.

Professor Popp's voice interrupted my thinking. "Wash your hands for dinner, children. Alex? Would you care to join us?"

I remembered Dad's stir-fry. "Yes!" I said. "Yes, I would!"

I was afraid Dad would argue when I phoned

to ask permission, but he said actually it might be better if I ate at Yasmeen's house. "That way if my stir-fry turns out to be lethal, you can say nice things at the funeral," he said.

"I'm sure your stir-fry will be delicious," I lied. "Is it okay if I'm home by eight? Yasmeen and I have some stuff to do after dinner."

"See you then," Dad said.

Dinner at the Popps' house was ham, mashed potatoes, and unidentifiable mushy green stuff. I cleaned my plate.

Mrs. Popp smiled at me. "It's a pleasure to feed such an appreciative guest."

"It's a pleasure to be here," I said sincerely.

Meanwhile, Jeremiah was trying the oldest trick in the book, talking to avoid eating. "Are you sure this is human food?" He poked the green stuff with his fork. "Because it looks like the food Miss Deirdre feeds Arnold."

"Jere*mi*ah?" Mrs. Popp said, warning him.

"Arnold is our class pet," Jeremiah explained to me.

"I believe he is a hamster," Professor Popp added.

"Uh-oh," Jeremiah said. "Did this ham come from a hamster?"

Professor Popp shook his head. "No hamsters were harmed in the making of this meal. So please finish your dinner, Jeremiah. It's good for you. Your body converts food to energy so you can play and jump and run around."

"Arnold runs around," Jeremiah said. "He has one of those running wheels. *Squeak! Squeak! Squeak!* Miss Deirdre has to take him home after school because he bothers the other people in the building."

"Vegetables are good for Arnold, too," Mrs. Popp said. "They're good for all God's creatures."

"What about ghosts?" Jeremiah asked. "Are vegetables good for ghosts?"

"There are no such things," Mrs. Popp said.

"Daddy believes in them," Jeremiah said.

"Do you, Daddy?" Yasmeen asked.

"I have studied the matter a little," he said, "and while I am skeptical, I am not necessarily an unbeliever."

"Oh, piffle!" said Mrs. Popp, and she stood up to clear the table.

"Can I ask you something," I said to Professor Popp, "since you've studied about ghosts?"

"You *may*." Professor Popp nodded.

"Why do they come back?" I asked. "I mean, not everybody who dies becomes a ghost, right? If they did, we'd be bumping into ghosts every minute."

"Most cultures believe that the shade, or ghost, has some unfinished work to attend to," Professor Popp said. "Often the deceased person has been accused of something unfairly, and its ghost seeks justice."

I thought about that. "So if a ghost was haunting somebody, then maybe the somebody should help the ghost out," I said.

Professor Popp wanted to know if I had something particular in mind, so I explained about Mr. Blanco and the Harvey house.

"Have you noticed a pattern to the ghostly appearances?" Professor Popp asked me.

"Come to think of it," I said, "it kind of

seems like they happen when people are talking about the ghost story."

"Then perhaps," Professor Popp said, "there's something in the story that the ghost doesn't like."

Yasmeen stacked my plate on top of her plate and Jeremiah's plate on top of mine. "So if that's true, it means Mr. Harvey *didn't* murder his wife," she said. "And his ghost won't settle down until he's proved innocent."

"I thought you didn't believe in ghosts," I said.

"Of course I don't," Yasmeen said. "But if there were ghosts, which there aren't, that would be the logical conclusion."

Chapter Twenty-five

After Yasmeen and I were done in the kitchen, there was time to take a look at the old black book and the newspapers from Mr. Blanco. In the family room Professor Popp was sitting on the sofa reading a yellow sheet of writing paper.

"I hope you don't mind." He looked up at us. "I was curious and opened this old ledger book. When I did, the stationery fluttered out. The handwriting is faded, but it seems to be a page from a *billet-doux*."

"A what?" I said.

"Oh, Daddy, how *romantic*!" Yasmeen said. "Let me see!"

Professor Popp handed her the paper. "*Billet-doux* is French for 'sweet note,'" he told me. "In English, a love letter. Where did you get all this?"

I told him, and he nodded. "It's a ledger book, quite a useful document for a historian." I didn't understand, so he explained that a careful man like Mr. Harvey would have written an entry for everything he bought and everything he earned in a ledger book. Professor Popp flipped through several pages. There were entries for lots of different purchases—big amounts for stuff like bricks and lumber, small amounts for flour, lamp oil, and ink.

"Are you sure this was Mr. Harvey's book?" I asked.

Professor Popp turned to the inside front cover. There, in spidery black writing, were the words: "Gilmore Samuel Harvey, July 1, 1877–"

"There's no ending date," I said.

"I noticed that, too," said Professor Popp. "Apparently his work was interrupted."

"What's the last entry?" I asked.

We paged through till we found it: On October 28, 1879, Samuel Harvey had purchased a "traveling portmanteau" from R. J. McClanahan's store for $3.50.

"What's a portmanteau?" I asked.

"Suitcase," Yasmeen said, without looking up from the page she was reading.

"I guess he never got to use it," I said. "He died on October thirty-first—I've seen his grave."

Yasmeen sighed a huge sigh, and when I looked at her face, it had this gross, dreamy expression. Usually I can forget that Yasmeen's a girl, but sometimes it is hard.

"This is so romantic!" she said. "Should I read it to you?"

"No," I said.

"Oh, come on," she said, *"please."*

"Give it over, and I'll read it myself," I said.

"It's only a piece of a longer letter," Professor Popp said. "I looked for more, but this is all that's here."

Frowning, Yasmeen handed me the sheet of stationery. It was so old it crinkled like it might shatter into confetti. I don't know how, exactly, but I could see right away that the writing was feminine. The letters were large and round, much different from Mr. Harvey's spidery black scrawl.

This must have been a middle page because it started midsentence:

> . . . *be with you always, dearest Floyd, but you know our circumstances make it impossible. We are star-crossed like the tragic lovers of yore. If only I had I met you sooner, if only my parents had been less bent on marrying off their old-maid daughter to a wealthy man, if only I had been a woman of some means of my own—were any of these "if onlys" satisfied, then I might have been your own Marianne. Alas, this will never . . .*

I looked up at Yasmeen. She still had the dreamy expression. "Listen, Yasmeen, this is really important, right? It confirms part of the story."

Yasmeen nodded. "It's from Marianne Harvey to stouthearted Floyd. It must be."

"Who?" Professor Popp said. "What?"

We explained that Mrs. Harvey was beautiful, that people said she had a sweetheart, and the sweetheart was the same guy who found her body, Floyd. Professor Popp nodded. "This would seem to confirm that there was a romance, and further, it would seem that she was calling an end to it. But I believe there may also be something more."

"What?" Yasmeen said.

"Consider *where* I found the letter," said Professor Popp. "It was tucked in the pages of Gilmore Harvey's ledger book. I haven't had a chance to look closely, but as far as I can tell, his is the only writing in the book. Do you see what I'm getting at?"

I nodded. "Gilmore Harvey was never supposed to see this letter—but he did, and that means he knew his wife had a sweetheart. And if he knew—well, then I guess it's the way the rumors said. That could be a reason to kill her."

"But now I'm not so sure he *did* kill her," Yasmeen said. "I mean—if Dad's right that ghosts come back seeking justice, what justice is his ghost seeking now?"

"Then there's the cat," I said. "Marianne's smart black cat, who supposedly killed Gilmore Harvey."

"It was a *cat* that killed Mr. Harvey?" Mr. Popp said.

"That's how the story goes," Yasmeen said. "Killed him in revenge after Mr. Harvey killed Marianne. And after that the cat was killed, too—drowned in the Harveys' well."

Mr. Popp shook his head. "Quite a gothic tale," he said. "But whatever the truth may be, you're not going to learn it on a school night."

I picked up the book and the newspapers. "Thanks for dinner," I said, "and for helping us."

On the short walk back home, my head was spinning. I was thinking about the receipt. I was thinking about the ledger book. But most of all I was thinking about that love letter.

Of course, knowing what happened to her, I felt totally terrible for beautiful Marianne Harvey. I mean, there she was, stuck with an old, ugly, mean husband and in love with a young guy who worked for him. I guess she must have been really unhappy. At the same time, though, hadn't she been unfair to her husband? I mean, once you get married, you aren't supposed to have sweethearts anymore.

But from the letter, it sounded like she was calling off the romance. So maybe she was trying to be good after all.

Luau met me at the front door and side-rubbed my leg, which meant, *Greetings, Alex. Believe it or not, my food bowl is empty!* I bent down and tickled him under his chin. "You know what, Luau?" I said. "You're lucky to be a cat."

Luau closed his eyes and purred, which meant, *And you're lucky to be a kid.*

Chapter Twenty-six

Apparently, the stir-fry did not kill my dad; he was standing in the kitchen.

"How did it taste?" I asked.

He pointed at the garbage disposal. "Rest in peace," he said. "But I'm pretty sure my culinary skills will improve when my eyes do. I took a double dose of the pills."

"Is that a good idea?" I asked. "What if you get X-ray vision?"

Dad threw a dish towel over his shoulder like a cape. "*Super*dad!"

I nodded. "Could come in handy solving crimes."

"Which reminds me," Dad said, "how goes the case of the missing cats?"

"Well, so far today, Yasmeen and I have realized that we're idiots," I said.

"That's not necessarily bad," Dad said. "Often, the first step toward wisdom is to recognize one's own foolishness."

"Is that from a fortune cookie?" I asked.

Dad said it might be, or he might have made it up. "When you get to be my age, it's not only your eyes that fail, it's your memory, too."

"You're not old, Dad," I said, which made him grin.

"Keep picking up your cues, Alex. Otherwise I'll have to hire a new sidekick."

I told Dad good night and took the old newspapers up to my room. Like the love letter, they were crinkly and yellow. It was weird to think how long they'd been around. Not a single person mentioned in them was still alive.

The two newspapers on the top were from 1876.

Then there was one from 1877. In them were articles about new buildings going up, streets being laid out, businesses opening. Most of the stuff was pretty boring.

And then I found it.

Page one, November 3, 1879.

HARVEY RITES TOMORROW
AT ST. BERNARD'S

I guess the newspaper reporters had already written about the murder itself because this article mostly talked about plans for the funeral and how important Mr. Harvey's business was. Toward the end the article reviewed the "peculiar circumstances" under which the body was found. From what this said, it looked like Mr. Stone's version of the story actually was right. The big black cat was found in the parlor with the body, the body had been so badly mauled it was "unrecognizable," Marianne Harvey had been strangled in the same room only two days before.

The last sentence read:

So bizarre and bloody a tragedy has never yet been heard of in the brief history of our fair town nor yet for many miles around.

I flipped through the rest of the papers quickly, but there was nothing else from 1879. I was about to turn out my light when I spotted a little tiny article at the bottom of the front page, easy to miss because the headline was small— like nobody thought it was important at the time.

And the way it turned out later, nobody in all the years since had thought it was important either.

Not till I did. But first there was the case of the missing cats to solve.

Chapter Twenty-seven

"Stouthearted Floyd disappeared?" Yasmeen repeated. We were on our way to school the next morning, Halloween day. "Right after Gilmore Harvey's body was found?"

"That's what the old newspaper said: 'One Floyd Anderson, an employee of Mr. Gilmore Harvey's dry goods emporium, was reported missing by his friends and colleagues.'"

Yasmeen thought for a minute. "Well, I suppose that might make sense," she said. "Probably he was afraid people would find out about him and Marianne Harvey. Probably he was afraid the police would suspect him of killing her husband, so he left town."

"Maybe," I said, "or maybe he was just so sad about her being dead that he ran away."

Sometimes, I swear, I can hear the wheels whirring in Yasmeen's head. This was one of those times. "What does it mean?" she muttered.

"I know," I said. "It's like the explanation is dangling right above us, but we can't jump high enough to reach it."

"It's been bad enough trying to find Halloween," Yasmeen said, "then you had to go and introduce a whole separate mystery."

"That is so unfair," I said. "You're the one who likes detecting. I never told Kyle we'd find his cat for him."

"Well, that, at least, we are going to do," she said. "Tonight—with a little help from Luau and Sophie."

Halloween used to be a fun day at school. We would have a costume parade and a class party. The teachers would read Halloween stories. But that all ended a couple of years ago when some parents complained that Halloween celebrates wickedness. Since then, October 31 has been a regular day like every other regular day. And this year it was worse than that, at least for Alex Parakeet, notorious abuser of his own cat. Only a person who has been hated by everyone in his entire school knows how bad that day was for me, knows how much I'd like to just forget it.

The only reason I even survived is I knew Monday would be better. Once Kyle's cat was home, Yasmeen would tell Billy Jensen the truth, Billy Jensen would tell the entire population of our town, and my life would go back to normal.

The three-o'clock bell finally rang, and I shot down the hallway and out the front doors. It was a few minutes before Sophie and Yasmeen came out to meet me. Sophie had something to show us: the radio collar for the undercover kitty. She smiled a huge smile when she pulled it out of her backpack.

"Try it out," she said, and handed me a receiver the size of a cell phone. Then she ran ahead a little ways and stopped. "Switch it on!"

she called. I pushed the button on the side. There were crackles and hisses, then Sophie's voice, kind of scratchy but plenty loud: "Can you hear me?"

"I can't believe it." I looked at Yasmeen. "She *is* a genius!"

Sophie was running back toward us by now and heard me. *"Duh,"* she said.

It annoys Yasmeen to discuss somebody else's genius, so she changed the subject. "What about the batteries?" she asked. "How long will they last?"

"Yeah, that might be a problem," Sophie said. "The one in the collar won't last that long. There's no way for a cat to switch it off, plus it's small. The ones in the receiver will probably go quite a while, but you might as well turn it off till we need it."

"*If* we need it," I said.

"Which we won't," Yasmeen said.

For once, Mom was home when I got there. She was in the family room, taking a break before going out on her Halloween patrol. I asked her whether any more cats were missing, and I was really glad when she said no.

"How was school today?" she asked.

The truthful answer would have been, "Terrible." But I didn't want to say that, because I didn't want her asking a bunch of questions. So I tried to think of something good and said, "I finished my map finally."

Mom smiled. "School hasn't changed in some ways," she said. "We made relief maps, too. I remember the dough left your hands all dried out."

I nodded. "Because there's so much salt in it. Salt, and flour, and . . . *Oh, my gosh.*"

I guess my face must have gone funny because Mom said, "Alex, are you okay?"

I nodded. I stood up. I said, "Kind of, Mom. I'm kind of okay. But I've got to call Yasmeen right now. I think I've just figured the whole thing out: I think I know the identity of the cat-napper!"

Chapter Twenty-eight

At the time I was ticked off at Mom for not taking my bright idea more seriously. But now I see it was probably good that she didn't—at least not right then. Instead of letting me call Yasmeen and instead of phoning dispatch and having Officer Krichels go arrest my new prime suspect, she sat me back down and made me explain what I had figured out.

When I got to the part about the grocery receipt, she said, "Wait one minute, Alex. Let's think this through, shall we? Chances are Mrs. Timmons *did* buy salt-dough ingredients. But there are other classes at your school making relief maps, right? So other teachers may have bought the ingredients as well. Are all those teachers catnappers?"

I sighed. Till that moment, I had never realized the journey from genius to idiot could be made so quickly. "Probably not," I said.

Mom got out her notebook and a pen. "Tell me the items on the receipt again," she said, and wrote down each one. Then, probably just to make me feel better, she asked, "Have you found out anything else?"

I thought of telling her about Prime Suspect No. 2—the mysterious Mr. Lee. But I didn't even have a grocery receipt's worth of evidence against him. So I just shook my head no.

"I'm frustrated, too," Mom said. "In fact, I'm almost hoping something happens tonight, something to blow the lid off the case once and for all."

Of course I knew something *was* going to happen that night. But I couldn't tell Mom about it. She would have put a stop to the whole thing, probably would even have called Yasmeen's parents and Sophie's parents, not to mention Mrs. Lee because it was her baby monitor we kind of borrowed when we were supposed to be taking it back to the store.

Yasmeen had said she was going to rest up this afternoon since we'd be awake practically all night. That sounded like a good idea to me, too. But before going upstairs, I took Luau's bed from its usual corner and put it out on the front porch so we'd be ready after trick-or-treating.

In my room, Luau was napping with his new catnip ball tucked under his ear like a pillow. I had the collar and the receiver in my backpack.

"Hey, lazy," I said. "Wake up."

Luau opened one eye and *mrrfed*, which meant, *You know, Alex, to us cats the word "lazy" is a compliment*. Then he saw the collar in my hand and stretched to give it a sniff. Usually he hates collars and tries to shake them off, but when I buckled this one around his neck, he sat up tall like a person proud of new clothes. I took a good look at the microphone, which was dangling from the ring where you were supposed to put a license. It looked like some fancy electronic beeper to scare birds. At least I hoped it did.

"Are you ready to catch a catnapper?" I asked Luau.

He bumped his head against my head, which meant, *Undercover Kitty at your disposal, sir.*

"Good man," I told him. "Now, move over."

A little before six, I was in the bathroom making final adjustments to my ears when someone rang the doorbell. On my way to answer it, I stopped in my bedroom to get the receiver, which I put in my sweatpants pocket. Luau followed me down the stairs and slipped outside when I opened the front door.

It was Yasmeen.

"You're early," I said. "Where's Jeremiah?"

"Coming." She was looking at her feet. "But first I wanted to warn you about something."

I had a bad feeling. "What?"

"It isn't just me and Jeremiah who are going trick-or-treating with you."

"Oh, no," I said. "Not . . ."

Yasmeen nodded, still looking at her feet. "Sophie asked and—after all she did—what was I supposed to say?"

I took a deep breath and let it out. "Okay," I said. "We'll deal."

A second later, Jeremiah and Sophie appeared on the sidewalk, walking toward our house. Sophie was wearing her angel costume, which featured real feathers and a light-up halo. Jeremiah was going as a peanut butter sandwich.

"Isn't that what he went as last year?" I asked Yasmeen, but she said no, last year he had been a jar of peanut butter.

"Trick or treat!" they shouted when they got to the door.

Mom came up behind me in the front hall. "Don't you guys look great!" she said.

"My costume's from a catalog," Sophie answered. "I got to pick whatever one I liked. I liked this because it was the most expensive. Do you want to know how much it cost?"

"Not especially," Mom said. "Come on in,

though. Would you prefer Tootsie Pops or pretzels?"

"Dumb question, Mom," I said.

Jeremiah and Yasmeen each took a Tootsie Pop and said thank you. Sophie took a handful of Tootsie Pops and forgot to say thank you.

Mom gave her a look. "You know, Sophie," she said, "there are going to be a lot more trick-or-treaters tonight."

"I know." Sophie nodded. "That's why I always go early, 'cause if you're late, you might get stuck with pretzels."

Whatever Mom wanted to say, I didn't want to hear. "Can we go now?" I asked quickly.

Mom nodded. "Trick-or-treating ends at eight, so you'll be back at a few minutes after, okay? I'll be working, but Dad will be home. And don't go beyond St. Bernard's on one side or the school on the other."

Just like I expected, things started out bad. Yasmeen, Jeremiah, and I *always* turn right at our front gate and hit the Blancos first. But Sophie said the Blancos had seaweed lollipops this year and we should skip them altogether. We were on the sidewalk in front of my house arguing when Mom called to us: "One more thing! The most important thing!"

I expected "Watch for catnappers" or "Be careful crossing streets," but what she actually said was, "Be sure to save me anything with coconut!"

We skipped the Blancos. At the Dagostinos we got peanut butter cups, and I gave mine to Jeremiah.

Mrs. Lee had forgotten to buy candy so she gave us each a handful of loose change. It must have come from the bottom of her purse because it had lint on it.

Mr. Stone gave us packets of cocoa mix.

And Bub had sugarless gum because, he said, he didn't want us kids to end up fat like him.

By the time we turned the corner onto Groundhog Drive, Sophie had accidentally kicked over two jack-o'-lanterns, but she was remembering to say thank you. Meanwhile, Jeremiah had taken a break from worrying to say he liked the light-up halo because cars could see it.

In other words things were going surprisingly well, which meant, as Jeremiah could have told you, that something was about to go wrong.

We had just turned onto Ari's front walk when Yasmeen said, "Hey, did I see your feline going outside when I came up to your door?"

I said, "Yeah, I guess. He likes to see what the squirrels are up to."

"Was that a good idea? Letting him out early?" Yasmeen asked.

"The catnapper never shows up till at least midnight, I thought," Sophie said.

"Catnapper?" Jeremiah said.

"Never mind," Yasmeen said. "Did you bring the receiver with you?"

"In my pocket," I said.

"Why don't you turn it on? Maybe we can figure out what the feline is doing."

Sophie said the batteries ought to be okay, so I held the receiver to my ear and pressed the button. At first there was only static. But then, suddenly, out of the tiny speaker blared a voice so loud it startled me, and I bobbled the receiver but caught it again. "Poor, pretty kitty. Are you cold? Yes, you are. Come on, pretty kitty, and I'll take you home."

"Whoa, it really does work!" said Yasmeen. "That's amazing!"

"But who was that talking?" I said.

"Your mom," said Sophie. "Wasn't it?"

Yasmeen laughed. "Mrs. Parakeet doesn't talk like—"

More noise from the speaker interrupted her. It sounded all rumbly like a car engine, but that wasn't quite right. It was a sound I recognized, though . . . what was it?

"Ohhh!" I laughed. "Luau's purring!"

"Whoever it is must've picked him up," said Yasmeen.

"Would somebody please tell me—" Jeremiah started to say.

But Sophie interrupted. "Wait a sec. If that lady who just picked up Luau *isn't* Alex's mom, then who is she?"

It hit me like a rock, and judging from Sophie's and Yasmeen's faces, it didn't feel so good to them either. Here we were grubbing for crunch bars door-to-door while, a couple of blocks away, my cat was in the process of being catnapped.

Talk about lousy cat owners. For this I'd make the Guinness Book.

Chapter Twenty-nine

"Will somebody please tell me—" Jeremiah tried again.

"It's the catnapper!" Sophie snapped. "The catnapper's a *girl*, and she's got Luau!"

Yasmeen is not real calm in a crisis. "Okay, okay," she said, but her voice had turned all breathless, the way voices do when you panic. "Everybody let's just sit down over here on the curb. Everybody, let's just try to keep calm. We don't know it's the catnapper. The catnapper *always* strikes after midnight. This is probably just some harmless lady taking Luau home. . . ."

The monitor crackled again, which—merci-fully—shut Yasmeen up, and through the speaker came the sound of a car starting.

"Oh, my gosh!" I moaned. "She could be tak-ing him anywhere. Sophie, quick, what do you think the range of the baby monitor is now?"

Sophie shook her head. "Hard to tell. I tested it to about a half mile; by then it was getting faint."

"So now," Yasmeen's panicky voice had gone all quiet and pathetic, "we are just going to sit here on the curb in front of Ari's house and lis-ten to Luau driving out of our lives forever like Halloween and those other cats, and it's all my fault, me with my brilliant plan, and—"

"No, it's not your fault," I said. "It's mine for letting him out. I never figured he'd be in danger so early—"

"Jeez, you two!" Sophie was disgusted. "Some kind of detectives you are. One little set-back and you give up! Well, I'm not giving up. What about you, Jeremiah?"

Jeremiah just shook his head. "Uh-oh," he said.

Without really noticing, we had been hearing the hum of the car engine through the speaker. Now, abruptly, it stopped, and then we heard the voice again, singsongy, but farther away, so we couldn't make out words. I wished to heck the monitor didn't distort sound so much. There was something familiar about the voice—it seemed like one I had heard before.

Rustling, bumping, slamming . . . what did all the sounds mean? Going from the car to the house? And then a double *thump* that maybe meant Luau was jumping to the ground. And finally something I recognized for sure, meowing. Lots of meowing. Was it one cat? Two cats? I couldn't tell.

"Is that Luau?" Yasmeen asked me. She was whispering.

"Uh-uh," I whispered. "Luau's meow is more drawn-out—you know."

Sophie said, "Plus the volume is wrong. I mean, Luau's mouth is only a couple of inches from the mike. Any noise he makes will be so loud it'll distort—probably be more like a shriek."

Sitting on the curb, I could feel the cold from the concrete rising right up my backbone. A group of kids I didn't know ran past on their way to Ari's. I envied them. They didn't have anything more important to worry about than whether Nestle's Crunch is better than Hershey's Krackel.

Without thinking, I turned to Sophie. "What do we do now?"

Sophie was decisive. "Sit and listen until we hear something to tell us where they are. Remember—they can't be too far away. If they were, we wouldn't be able to hear them."

"It would be good if you had taught Luau to talk," Jeremiah said. "Then he could just whisper a street number into the mike."

Yasmeen started to answer, but a blast of sound from the monitor interrupted her—and almost blew out all eight of our eardrums.

"*That* was Luau's meow!" Sophie said.

"What was he saying?" Yasmeen asked.

"I can't understand him," I said. "I don't think it was an address."

"Say it again, Luau." Yasmeen spoke into the receiver like it worked both ways.

The chorus of meowing continued, with Luau apparently keeping quiet this time. I thought I could pick out at least two other cats. One had a small, high-pitched meow, while the other's was gruff and squeaky, like a rusty hinge.

A rusty hinge. Why did that seem familiar? Had somebody said something once about a cat . . . ?

"Hey—wait!" I said. "I *know* one of those cats! It's Halloween!"

Yasmeen frowned. "What do you mean?" she said. "You never even met Halloween."

"But remember," I said, "the time we went over to Kyle's? He said Halloween had a funny meow. And that's it—I know it is."

Yasmeen nodded slowly, then faster, as if one piece of good news was just what she needed to shake her into action. "I do remember," she said.

"We're going to get them back," I said.

Yasmeen nodded, and Sophie smiled. "Well, that's better. Give me over the receiver a sec, Alex. I want to take a look at—" Sophie grabbed for it, but at the same time I heard the voice again and jerked it back to listen. I don't know whose fault it was—well, yes, I do, it was Sophie's—but next thing the receiver dropped to the street, bounced once, and broke in two.

Chapter Thirty

For a moment we all stood staring at the broken, silent receiver. Then Jeremiah said, "Nice move, foofoo-heads."

"We can fix it—maybe," Sophie said. "All I need is—"

I looked up at her, and it was like my body decided to spit out all the anger and worry and frustration that had built up since we started trying to find Halloween. *You broke it!* I shouted. "We *never* should've let you help!"

Yasmeen put her hand on my shoulder. "Alex," she said, "that wasn't fair."

I shook her hand off. "Leave me alone," I

said. "Anyway,"—my face was wet with tears and snot. I sniffed some back and wiped the rest—"it's too late."

They all looked at me.

"Because of what the catnapper was saying," I went on, "right before it broke."

"What was she saying?" Yasmeen asked.

It was hard even to get the words out—they were that creepy. "She said,"—I took a breath, and my voice shook—"'C'mere, kitty, this won't hurt. You're just going night-night now.'"

"Oh, no," Yasmeen said.

Sophie picked up the broken receiver and studied it. "Nothing inside's busted, I don't think. If I had some way to stick it together, I could probably get it working."

"There's no time!" I said. "Luau's in la-la land by now, and who knows what awful thing the catnapper is doing to him!"

While I was talking, Yasmeen was tugging the bottom of her fat bumblebee costume up over her waist, trying to reach something in the pocket of the jeans underneath. If this hadn't been one of the two or three most terrible moments of my life, I would have cracked up because she looked extremely ridiculous.

"What are you doing?" I said.

Her answer was to brandish the Band-Aids she always keeps with her. "Will these work?" she asked Sophie.

"Yeah—yeah, probably. Give 'em over." Sophie grabbed and a second later had ripped three Band-Aids open. Their wrappers fluttered to earth, and Jeremiah, who would never be a litterbug, retrieved them. Meanwhile, Sophie wrapped the Band-Aids around the receiver and pressed the switch. Instantly, there was a jumble of squawks, shrieks, and hisses.

What was going on?

"Maybe the receiver's still broken?" I said.

Sophie shook her head. "No, it's working okay. Whatever we're hearing"—she took an anxious breath—"that's what's happening to Luau."

The noises were awful. Bumping, crashing, glass breaking. The constant squawk and hiss. Every once in a while, like an exclamation point, the earsplitting shriek that was Luau's meow.

It took Jeremiah to point out something totally obvious: "That doesn't sound like sleeping."

Relief flooded over me. "Of course!" I said. "That's what's happening—Luau is running from her. We're hearing the chase scene!"

"Run, Luau, run!" Yasmeen said, and Sophie and Jeremiah joined in.

"Shhh," I said. "Listen. What's that? A new noise . . ." This one was a rhythmic squeak. It had started slow—*squeak*, pause, *squeak*, pause, *squeak*, and then gotten faster—*squeak*, *squeak*, *squeak*, and now *sque-sque-sque*. . . . This was so hard, trying to understand what was going on only from sounds. This sound was familiar, but what did it remind me of? I scrinched up my eyes and concentrated, looking for the matching memory in my brain. I couldn't find it.

But Jeremiah could. "That's Arnold," he said simply.

Sophie, Yasmeen, and I looked at him, not understanding. "Jeremiah?"

"You know, our class pet. The hamster. That's him. That's his wheel."

Chapter Thirty-one

In your whole life you have never seen a cat, a bumblebee, an angel, and a peanut butter sandwich run as fast as we did. In fact, I was standing, out of breath, on Miss Deirdre's front porch before I had time to think about what I was supposed to do when I got there.

Sophie still had the receiver—now so close to the transmitter, the sound was really clear. Knowing at last who the catnapper was, I couldn't believe I hadn't recognized her sing-songy voice sooner.

She was speaking now: "That's it, kitty cat. Stay right there. Now I've got you."

"Ring the bell! Ring the bell! Hurry!" I said.

Sophie punched the button with her fist. The result was weird: We heard the bell ring indoors through the receiver at the same time we heard it ring outdoors in real life. And then we heard Miss Deirdre say, "*Drat*—what a time for trick-or-treaters!"

"Turn off the receiver!" Yasmeen whispered to Sophie, who quickly pressed the button.

And then the door opened.

I'm not sure what I expected. I guess I thought Miss Deirdre would look all of a sudden gigantic, or monstrous, or scary. But instead, standing in the doorway smiling brightly, she was plain old Miss Deirdre, the ditzy preschool teacher, Marjie Lee's nice friend who lived around the corner. It was totally hard to get that she was also the person who stole all those cats, who stole *my* cat, the person who a few minutes ago was threatening to send Luau "night-night."

"My, aren't the four of you darling!" she said to us. "Isn't that my little Jeremiah? And your sister and her friend, too! And what's your name, dear?"

"Sophie Sikora," Sophie answered.

"Well, you're a dear little angel, and I bet you're hoping for some treats, aren't you?"

"Yes, ma'am," said Sophie. "Only . . . I hope you don't mind, but Jeremiah's got to use the bathroom really, *really* bad. Can we come in?"

Jeremiah looked up at Sophie. "No, I don't have to—"

To shut him up, Sophie patted his head, only it was more like she thumped him. "I know it's embarrassing, Jeremiah, but she's your teacher, right? She knows about this kind of junk." Then she smiled up at Miss Deirdre, whose own smile was all of a sudden pretty fake looking.

"Uhhhh . . . ," Miss Deirdre said. "Well, of course, I *am* a child development professional, but my house is at sixes and sevens right now, and—"

"That's okay. My mother"—using Jeremiah as a battering ram, Sophie pushed past Miss Deirdre and into the house, talking all the while—"is a terrible housekeeper! Do you have cats? We have a cat. And her fur . . ."

Yasmeen and I, full of admiration, couldn't do anything but follow.

Inside, Miss Deirdre's smile disappeared and

her eyes darted corner to corner. From the stand next to the front door, she pulled a big black umbrella, then held it by her side.

Sophie pretended not to notice anything strange. "Bathroom's uh . . . *that way,* huh?" she said, and shoved Jeremiah ahead of her.

"Wait! No!" Miss Deirdre said.

Sophie paid no attention to her, just kept walking toward the back of the house. Most of the lights were off, but there was a room on the right that was all lit up. Through the doorway I could see it didn't have regular furniture in it but counters and stools, and on the counters were glittering glass containers of all sizes. I didn't see more, because Miss Deirdre dashed ahead of us and slammed the door shut.

"The bathroom," she said, shooing us back toward the front door, "is down *that* hallway and—"

She never finished giving directions. From below us came a for-real caterwauling like you wouldn't believe. And leading the chorus was a familiar voice, my own Luau, the undercover kitty: *It's about time you got here, guys! We felines in the basement could use a bit of rescue!*

Miss Deirdre's rosy cheeks went pale, but she wasn't giving in. "Only my kitties." She tried to smile. "You'll just excuse me a minute, children, while I gather them up? You see, they're not well socialized. I wouldn't want any precious children to be scratched."

"That's okay," Sophie said. "We *love* cats."

Desperate, Miss Deirdre ceased to be the so-sweet preschool teacher. Her eyes flared, and she held up the umbrella like a weapon. "You two stop *now*. No more nonsense."

The change in Miss Deirdre even intimidated Sophie. She stopped in her tracks and pulled Jeremiah close to protect him.

Would Miss Deirdre really have conked Sophie with the umbrella?

Would she have catnapped *us*?

Or would Sophie have displayed unexpected martial arts skills that saved the day?

I will never know because two things happened, one right after the other.

The first cracked all us kids up—and you can't simultaneously battle a catnapping pre-school teacher and crack up.

Through a doorway at the far end of the house came six cats, single file. The last in line was Luau, looking like his big-shouldered, muscley self. The others—well, they were the hilarious part. Each one was wearing his own little rainbow sweater, for one thing. And underneath, from tip of nose to tip of tail, each was as bald and pink as a watermelon jelly bean.

The other thing that happened was Mom. Lights flashing and siren blaring, she pulled up outside—with Officer Krichels right behind her.

Chapter Thirty-two

No surprise that Mom had a lot of questions for Miss Deirdre. But Miss Deirdre wouldn't talk without a lawyer. So Officer Krichels drove her downtown to the police station. Then Mom called Sophie's parents and the Popps.

"They're fine," she said into the phone. "I'll bring them home as soon as animal control comes for the cats."

While we waited for Mom, Yasmeen, Sophie, Jeremiah, and I sat on the sofa in Miss Deirdre's family room, bald kitties draped all over us, snuggling for warmth. At first, it had been more than creepy to touch these strange alien creatures in their fuzzy rainbow sweaters, but now we were getting used to it. If you focused on their eyes, you could almost remember they were cats.

"I have thought and thought, and I still can't figure out what Miss Deirdre was doing," Yasmeen said. "Why did she shave them?"

"Why did she steal them in the first place?" Sophie said.

"I'm just glad nobody's pushing me around anymore," Jeremiah said, glaring at Sophie.

"I'm sorry, kid, but it was an emergency," she said.

"I thought you were really brave," I told her.

Sophie looked at me, like she expected me to say more.

"And I am really sorry," I said. "I didn't mean it when I said we shouldn't have let you help. I was just so frustrated. I thought I was never going to get Luau back."

Luau twisted in my lap and looked up at me, which meant, *That would be enough to drive anyone over the edge.*

Sophie looked like she didn't think I was quite sorry enough. "Okay, I guess," she said. "But it was a terrible thing to say after all the work I did. And I had to spend my own money at the hardware store, too. I had to buy—" She started to detail the teensy-weensy parts she had purchased to transform the baby monitor, and all their prices. It was not very interesting, so I interrupted her.

"Did anybody else notice that weird room? Miss Deirdre sure closed the door fast."

Yasmeen moved the kitties on her lap aside, stood up, and grinned. "Who else wants to take a look?"

"I'm in," I said. "Mom's still on the phone. Don't touch anything, Sophie."

The room was toward the back of the house. I pulled my sleeve over my hand so I wouldn't get fingerprints on the knob. When I opened the door, the lights were still on.

"What *is* all this stuff?" I asked.

Yasmeen was looking around, shaking her head. "I know what it looks like," she said. "A laboratory. My aunt works in one at the hospital." She pointed at a machine that looked like a mini-merry-go-round. "That's a centrifuge," she said. "And this one is an autoclave—for sterilizing test tubes and stuff."

"What I don't get is why a preschool teacher would have a room like this in her house," Sophie said. "It's like she was a mad scientist or something."

"She made really good play dough," Jeremiah said.

I walked farther inside. On one counter I found Ziplocs full of dried green stuff like the herbs Bub keeps for soup. On a shelf above these were three larger Ziplocs full of something that looked like white fur. Next to these was a cardboard box labeled GEL CAPSULES and a neat row of yellow pill bottles.

"These are like the ones my dad got from Mr. Blanco," I said.

Then I looked again. Were they *like* the ones my dad got from Mr. Blanco? Or were they the *very same ones* my dad got from Mr. Blanco?

A second later, I had my answer. "What does

this say?" Jeremiah held up a white label printed with black letters.

Yasmeen read over his shoulder. "HOMESPUN REMEDIES—EYESIGHT."

And suddenly the whole thing made sense— more or less. We were standing in the lab where my dad's eyesight pills were manufactured. And what were they manufactured from? Cat fur, that's what! Miss Deirdre was stealing cats, shaving them, and using their fur as an ingredient in the pills. Cats have great eyesight, so the homespun idea would be that a dose of their fur would improve people's eyes, too.

It was a pretty lame idea, and I couldn't say I was real surprised that Dad's eyes were as bad as ever. I smiled when I thought of what he would say when he found out his miracle pills were full of cat fur.

In the cafeteria the other day, Yasmeen had promised Kyle that she wouldn't bring his cat, Halloween, back to him. So when we went to Kyle's front door later that night, I held Halloween and

Yasmeen stood innocently beside us. Sophie and Jeremiah had already gone home. Mom was in her police car waiting for us at the curb.

"Are you sure this is a good idea?" Yasmeen asked. "I mean, Kyle seems like kind of a delicate kid. Seeing his cat in this condition could give him a heart attack."

Halloween meowed her rusty-hinge meow. Ugly as she was, she did seem to be a good cat. I wondered if she knew how she looked and if she cared.

"I don't know about Kyle," I said, "but after what she's been through, this poor kitty shouldn't have to go to the pound overnight. She deserves to be home."

The door opened and a lady—Kyle's mom, I guess—was on the other side. "It's awfully late for trick-or-treating," she said. Then she spotted Halloween and shuddered. *"Oh, dear,"* she said. "A pet rat wearing a *sweater!*"

Kyle came up behind her then, and right behind him—what a surprise—was Cammie. Kyle looked at Halloween, looked at me, looked at Halloween, and then eagerly reached for her. "What happened to you, pal?" he said as he pulled the cat close.

Yasmeen couldn't believe it. "How did you even recognize her?" she asked.

"A man knows his own cat," Kyle said.

"Oh, my gracious, don't tell me that poor, hideous creature is—" his mom said.

"Halloween!" Cammie hollered. "Cool! Can we take the sweater off? I always wanted to know what cats look like naked!"

Chapter Thirty-three

Mom didn't ask us a lot of questions Halloween night. She was concentrating on Miss Deirdre and the bald kitties. But when she and I were sitting at the breakfast table the next morning, it all came out—how we had borrowed the baby monitor and Sophie had turned it into a wire for Luau, how we had used Luau as catnapper bait.

Like I predicted, Mom was not totally thrilled with our methods.

"The baby monitor didn't belong to you in the first place," she said.

"I know that, Mom."

"And what right had you to put your cat at risk?" Mom nodded at Luau. He had been snoozing on his cushion under the counter, but when he heard *cat*, he looked up. "A poor, dumb animal," Mom went on, "who can't speak for himself."

"A poor, dumb animal?" I said. "Mom, he volunteered!"

Mom sipped her coffee. "Right," she said.

Luau interrupted with a meow. He had padded over to sit by Mom's chair. Now he leaped lightly into her lap and started circling.

"He's telling you it was his idea," I said.

"Oh, is he?" Mom said. "I thought he was telling me there's a new box of cat treats in the cupboard."

"I don't see how he can say it any more clearly. He *liked* being the undercover kitty. He was proud to serve his fellow felines."

Mom stroked Luau. "Have it your way," she said. "But about that baby monitor, how much have you got saved?"

Oh, this was just great. Here Yasmeen and

I had solved the crime, caught the catnapper, returned Kyle's cat—and instead of getting a reward, it was going to cost me cold, hard cash.

I sighed. "If I use my birthday money," I said, "I've probably got enough to pay Mrs. Lee back."

"Good."

It seemed like a smart idea to change the subject. So I asked Mom what she had found out from Miss Deirdre. "Was I right?" I said. "Was she making those pills for Mr. Blanco?"

Mom nodded. "She's an animal lover big-time, and she got interested in these alternative kinds of cures after she read some book about homespun remedies. Her idea was that she could do well by doing good."

"What does that mean?"

"She thought she could rescue neglected cats and make money at the same time," Mom said.

"Wasn't she scared when she was stealing the cats?" I asked. "She almost got caught a couple of times."

Mom smiled. "That was her big inspiration.

You know, I think maybe Miss Deirdre was such a successful teacher because she's a kid at heart. For example, she loved to play dress-up."

"You mean she had a costume for cat-napping?"

"More like a disguise," Mom said. "She knew how the Harvey ghost was supposed to steal cats at Halloween. So she decided to confuse matters by transforming *herself* into a ghost. And I don't mean she wore some cheesy old sheet either. She had gray face makeup and a veil, and her dress was more like a gauzy gray gown."

"Doesn't sound good for fast getaways," I said.

"She made it short so she wouldn't trip," Mom said. "She wore gray tights and running shoes with it. I guess she was pretty proud of the costume. Even though she was sitting in a police station, she wanted to tell me all about it."

I said I thought it was too bad Miss Deirdre had turned out to be a bad guy. "She's good at a lot of things. How did she make the pills, anyway?"

"Apparently, she collected the fur, bleached it white, ground it into a powder, and put the powder into the gel capsules."

"Did she really think they would work?" I asked. "I mean—*ick*—swallowing cat fur? Poor Dad!"

Mom laughed. "Well, she added herbs, so it was tasty cat fur, at least, and clean, too. But your dad told me early this morning he's pretty embarrassed. In fact, he's at the eye doctor now."

"Is Mr. Blanco going to get in trouble?" I asked. "It seems like maybe there would be a law against selling pills made out of cat fur."

"The district attorney says it's not the kind of consumer fraud case he's used to," Mom said, "so he's still looking into it. There was no real harm done, so my bet is Mr. Blanco will get off with a slap on the wrist."

"The D.A. is going to slap Mr. Blanco's wrist?"

"Not literally, Alex," Mom said. "It just means the punishment won't be too severe. At the very least, Mr. Blanco will have to return

Daddy's money and promise to be more careful about what he sells in the future." She took another sip of coffee and stretched. Luau had to hold tight to keep from falling out of her lap. "You know," she said, "I'm going downtown to question Miss Deirdre again later, and there are still a few things I don't understand."

"No prob, Mom. After talking to Kyle last night, I've got it all figured out."

"In that case," she said, "why did Kyle call you and Yasmeen off the case? Was Bub right? Was there a ransom note?"

I shook my head no. "It was the ghost," I said.

"You mean Miss Deirdre dressed up," Mom said.

"No," I said, "I mean the *real* ghost. Kyle was at the Harvey house on Sunday buying catnip. He hoped maybe he could use it to lure Halloween home. Anyway, when he was there, the ghost of Gilmore Harvey started making noise—"

"The ghost of Gilmore Harvey started making noise?" Mom repeated.

"The ghost makes noise, Mom. Trust me. Anyway, Kyle became convinced it was the ghost who stole Halloween."

Mom said that was no wonder. "He's a morbid kid, anyway, and he saw Miss Deirdre in full regalia when she stole his cat."

I nodded. "Anyway, when that happened, he was afraid it was a warning that he should stop looking. He didn't want anything bad to happen to Yasmeen and me, so he called us off, too."

"He's a Gloomy Gus, all right," Mom said. "And I guess that also explains why he put the LOST flyer in the cemetery in the first place."

"You got it," I said. "He was hoping the ghost would see it and return the cat. Hey—but can I ask *you* something? How did *you* figure out about Miss Deirdre—that she was the catnapper? It was sure lucky you and Officer Krichels arrived when you did."

"Luck nothing." Mom smiled. "It was superior police work and my brilliant powers of deduction."

"That's what I meant to say. So how did you do it?"

"The grocery receipt," she said. "Mrs. Timmons isn't the only one who makes salt dough. I reread my notes from questioning Kyle. Cammie told me she had just made a unicorn out of play dough at school. Play dough, salt dough . . . It seemed like it was worth asking Miss Deirdre a few questions at least."

"And the next thing you knew, you were organizing a bald-cat rescue mission."

"Righty-o," Mom said, "and this morning I've got a date with a catnapper and her lawyer. Your dad, on the other hand, will be spending a pleasant day cleaning the basement. Care to join him?"

I had kind of thought since Yasmeen and I solved the crime and all, maybe we could celebrate. I mean, weren't we sort of heroes? But apparently, Mom didn't see it that way. She probably wondered why I sounded sarcastic when I answered her. "You know I'd love to, Mom, but I have some errands to run."

"What errands?" she asked.

I told her Yasmeen and I were going over to

Mr. Blanco's store to return the ledger book and the old newspapers, but on the way we were stopping at Bub's. We wanted to fill him in on who stole Halloween and see if he had any ideas about the other mystery: What had really happened on that Halloween more than a century ago? Was it true Gilmore Harvey was murdered by his very own cat?

"I thought you and Yasmeen were done with mysteries for a while," Mom said.

"We were till last night," I said, "but solving one kind of gives you energy for another."

"I know what you mean. And anyway, Dad will be happy to save you one of the grungier jobs. We wouldn't want you to feel left out."

Instead of answering, I retrieved my coat from the front hall. Mom started upstairs to get dressed, but she stopped halfway. "Speaking of breakfast," she said, "did you get any coconut candy last night?"

"Sorry, Mom," I said. "We weren't out long enough. But you're a grown-up. You can buy all the coconut candy you want."

"That would be cheating," Mom said. "Oh—and one more thing."

I pushed open the front door. "Yeah?"

"You and Yasmeen did okay, Alex. For kids, I mean."

Chapter Thirty-four

Bub was in the kitchen chopping celery for soup when Yasmeen and I arrived a little later. "I hear you two caught a catnapper last night," he said. "Not too high and mighty this morning to help a fella do dishes I hope?"

I was thinking "congratulations" might be nice, or simply, "I bet that kid was happy to get his cat back." But praise is not Bub's style, just like it's not my mom's. So I took a dishrag and turned on the water while Yasmeen pulled a drying towel out of the drawer. While we worked, we told Bub the latest about Miss Deirdre and the pills. Then we told him we had brought over the evidence from the other mystery—the case of the Harvey house ghost. When the last pan was clean, Bub put the lid on the soup pot and lowered the heat. Then we went into the front room and sat down at the dining room table, with the old ledger book, the billet doux, and the newspapers laid out in front of us.

Bub said he didn't know how it worked in real life, that I'd have to ask my mom about that, but in books and movies when the detectives were stuck, they usually reviewed the story one more time.

"It's worth a try," I said.

Bub nodded. "Okay, then. It's 1879 and the richest guy in town, one Gilmore Harvey, finds out his beautiful young wife has a sweetheart, Floyd. So—in the proverbial jealous rage—he kills her."

"Right before Halloween," Yasmeen added.

Bub nodded. "Then on Halloween night itself, someone—or some *thing*—kills Mr. Harvey."

"Right," I said. "And when the police find his body, they find Mrs. Harvey's cat at the same time—"

"Licking something red and sticky from his paws." Yasmeen made a face.

"So they blame the cat for killing Mr. Harvey," Bub said. "Now, here, come to think of it, I have a question. Did they blame the cat just because of the red stuff on his paws? Or was there some other reason?"

"It's just like you always say, Bub: means, motive, opportunity. The cat was there in the room, so that's opportunity. The cat wanted revenge for the death of his mistress, so that's motive. And as for means—well, apparently, the cat had some mighty big claws."

"According to Mr. Stone," Yasmeen said, "the body was so badly mauled it was like an attack by a 'jungle beast.' You couldn't even tell who the person was anymore."

Something about what Yasmeen just said struck me funny, like it was illogical. It was a few seconds before I realized what. "If you couldn't recognize the body . . . ," I said slowly, "how did anybody even know the body *was* Mr. Harvey?"

"Well, they knew because . . ." Yasmeen said, and then she stopped. "I don't know how they knew."

"In those days they wouldn't have the chemical tests they do now," Bub said. "They probably would have identified him by his clothes."

Clothes, I thought. Hadn't somebody said something about clothes not so long ago?

When it came to me—and when at the same time a lot of other things made sense, too—I was so excited I jumped out of my chair: *"The burned clothes in the parlor fireplace!"*

Yasmeen was annoyingly calm. "What burned clothes in what parlor fireplace?"

"I never told you," I said, "because it didn't seem important compared with the ledger and the love letter and all."

"Tell me now," Yasmeen said, and I explained how Mr. Blanco had found the old fireplace behind a wall, how he had saved the burned-up contents in a Ziploc bag, how it looked like maybe somebody had burned clothes in there. "Listen," I said finally. "I don't think it was Mr. Harvey at all who died on Halloween night. I think it was stouthearted Floyd. And the cat wasn't the killer either. Mr. Harvey was."

Bub offered to drive Yasmeen and me to the Harvey house on his way to the grocery store, but he needed to make out his shopping list first, and we didn't want to wait. "Promise me a full report," he said. And out the door we ran.

At the Harvey house, Mrs. Blanco was working the cash register. She didn't say hello. She started apologizing, but I was so focused on getting hold of that Ziploc bag that I didn't understand. Then I remembered the cat pills. In fact, I was kind of mad at her and Mr. Blanco for selling them, but I didn't think they deserved worse than what my mom had called a slap on the wrist either.

"Mrs. Blanco?" I interrupted her mid-sorry. "Yasmeen and I actually came about something different. Would it be okay if we took a look at the plastic bag of black stuff from the fireplace? We can take it out in the yard, if that's okay."

The bag was still behind the counter, and Mrs. Blanco was very happy to hand it over. I think she would have handed over the money from the cash register, too, if I had asked her—anything to show how sorry she was. "You'll need these," she said, handing us each a pair of rubber gloves. "We keep them for scrubbing. Oh—and take some newspaper. You can pour the contents out onto it."

It was a cool day, so we sat in the sunshine on the grass where the pumpkins had been. I put on my gloves, and Yasmeen put on hers. We looked at each other, then I picked up the bag, unzipped it, and dumped it out.

"Yuk," Yasmeen said, and I sneezed. Black dust floated all around us, and the burned smell was terrible—even after more than a century. It didn't take us long to get over the *yuk*, though, because what was inside the bag was interesting. Poking around among the black lumps, we found pieces of leather that might have come from someone's shoes, several blackened pieces of cloth, and a hard, round thing, heavier than the leather, that we couldn't identify at all.

"Rub it," Yasmeen said. "See if any of the black will come off."

I tore a page from the newspaper, wadded it

up, spit on it, and started to rub. I expected Yasmeen to be grossed out by my spit, but she wasn't, which shows that her curiosity was pretty overwhelming.

Feeling a little like Aladdin with his lamp, I rubbed—and in a short while, I could see that the thing was made of metal, and in another short while that it was silver. In the sunshine it winked at me.

"It's a pocket watch!" Yasmeen said.

"The back of one, I think. The glass and the face must have burned up—or melted."

"Keep rubbing!" Yasmeen said, as if I needed to be told. "Wouldn't it be cool if—"

I nodded and finished her thought. "If there was writing on it or something. Like: 'To my darling Floyd, Yours always, Marianne.'"

"Does it say that?"

"No," I said, and Yasmeen's face fell. "But take a look at what it does say."

The surface of the watch was pretty clean, but the three letters etched into the metal had stayed grimy black, easy to read.

"Who's F.A.S.?" Yasmeen said.

"I don't know," I said. "I mean the *F* could be Floyd, but his last name was Anderson—*A*, not *S*."

Yasmeen took the watch from me, studied it for a minute, and started laughing. That was weird by itself, but then she said, "My parents have these fancy towels they put out for guests," which was totally weird.

"Are you feeling okay?" I asked.

She ignored my question. "See here how the *A* in the middle is so much bigger than the other two letters?" she asked. "That's how it is on the towels, too—only on the towels it's the *P* for Popp, the last name. Do you get it? It's how old-fashioned monograms work. So the *S* on the right would've been Floyd's middle name. And the big *A* is for Anderson." Yasmeen nodded. "This is his monogram all right, and that makes this his watch, too."

Chapter Thirty-five

Back inside, Mrs. Blanco asked if we had learned anything.

"The watch belonged to Floyd after all," I said.

I could see from the way she nodded that Mrs. Blanco had no idea what I was talking about. "Why don't you two wash your hands and go tell that to Mr. Blanco?" she said. "He's working in the attic. I'm sure he'd be interested."

We had to go up two flights of stairs, the second one narrow, creaky, and dark. We could hear a roar above us. What in the world was that? Had the ghost learned a new trick?

A trapdoor led to the attic itself. Feeling apprehensive, I pushed up on it and climbed through with Yasmeen behind me. We saw right away that the roar was only a vacuum cleaner. Mr. Blanco was on his knees suctioning out the vents around the edge of the roof. Leaves were flying everywhere. I had to tap him on the shoulder before he noticed us.

Like his wife, he was totally apologetic: "Deirdre told me she was getting those pills from a pharmaceutical company. I had no idea she was cooking them up in her spare bedroom!"

"I hope that all works out okay," I said. "But what we really came to tell you is that Yasmeen and I figured out the mystery of the Harvey house ghost."

If I do say so myself, Yasmeen and I did a smooth job telling the story. It might not have been as elegant and spooky as Mr. Stone's version, but maybe if it were told over and over for one hundred years, it would be. We started the same way Bub had earlier. In 1879 a rich man named Gilmore Harvey found out his beautiful wife, Marianne, had a sweetheart, an employee of his named Floyd Anderson. In a jealous rage Mr. Harvey killed his wife a few nights before Halloween, then blamed her death on a burglar. The body was discovered by Floyd. So far, this was the same as Mr. Stone's version. But then the truth and the story diverged.

"Probably Mr. Harvey was afraid the police would catch him eventually, so he came up with a clever plan. He decided to fake his own death," I said. "First, he bought a suitcase. Then, somehow he got Floyd to come over on Halloween night. I guess that wouldn't have been hard—he was Floyd's boss. And when Floyd did, he killed him. Then . . ." I shuddered. This part was so grisly I didn't want to think about it. "Then he put his own clothes on Floyd and made it look like a wild animal had attacked him with its claws."

"A wild animal or a wild cat wanting revenge," Yasmeen said, "Marianne's pet cat."

" 'Black as midnight, with eyes as green and bright as emeralds,' " I quoted from Mr. Stone's story, " 'found by the hearth, cleaning something red and sticky from its paws.' "

Yasmeen sighed. "Poor cat."

"Yeah," I nodded. "Poor cat. Mr. Harvey *framed* him! I guess he hated the cat like he hated Marianne. He must have even put blood on the cat's paws, so naturally, any cat would lick it off. And when the police found the body, that's what the cat was doing."

"It looked like the cat was the killer," Yasmeen said, "and I guess with its being Halloween and everything, such a supernatural kind of a story seemed more believable than it would've any other day."

"So the clothes I found in the fireplace?" Mr. Blanco said.

"They were Floyd's," Yasmeen said, and she showed what was left of the pocket watch to Mr. Blanco.

"Gilmore Harvey burned them, only he was in a hurry and didn't do that great a job," I said. "After that, he took his new portmanteau and he left town—never to return."

"There's one other thing, though." Yasmeen looked around the attic. It was dusty and dim, with crates and boxes everywhere. I bet there were a zillion clues to a zillion mysteries in that attic. But as far as what happened in the Harvey house—that one we had solved, hadn't we?

"There's no other thing," I said. "We have it all figured out. We are great detectives." Heck, if no one else was going to make a fuss over what a good job we'd done, I would do it myself.

"Oh, yes, there is," Yasmeen said. "The ghost. Dad said ghosts usually come back because there's unfinished business, some kind of injustice. But that doesn't fit, does it? Mr. Harvey got his revenge, *and* he got away with it. For that matter, his ghost, if he's got one, wouldn't be hanging around here. It would be hanging around wherever Mr. Harvey himself ended up dying, wouldn't it?"

"So what are you saying?" I said. "It's *not* Mr. Harvey's ghost that haunts the Harvey house?"

"That's what I'm saying," she said.

"Then whose ghost is—" I started to ask, but Mr. Blanco interrupted me.

"Uh, kids?" he said. "Actually, about the ghost. There isn't one."

"What?" Yasmeen and I said at the same time. "But we've seen it," I said. "Well, heard it anyway."

"Sorry to disappoint you," Mr. Blanco said, "but today's the first day I've come up here into the attic to work, and you wouldn't believe the funky stuff—electrical wiring like nobody ever saw. And with the vents half blocked and the wind blowing through. Well, I'm not surprised we've been hearing noises downstairs."

"You mean the yowling?" I said.

"Now that I've taken a look around up here, it's all easily explained," he said. "No need to bring in the spirit world. The wind blows a certain way through these half-clogged vents—it whistles, and this attic becomes an echo chamber. Plus the wires up here get blown around, too. And that disrupts the electrical connections."

"So the lights flash," I said, "and then they go out?"

"Exactly," he said. "Anyway, I'm thinking the ghost is gone for good. I'm getting these vents cleared today, and I've got an electrician coming on Monday."

Yasmeen made a face. She wasn't buying Mr. Blanco's explanation. It was funny that till lately she never believed in ghosts. Now all of a sudden she seemed kind of attached to them. "I have a different theory," she said.

Mr. Blanco smiled. "Okay, shoot."

"There's a ghost all right, but it's not Mr. Harvey," she said.

"Floyd then?" I said. "Or Marianne?"

Yasmeen shook her head. "What happened to them was tragic, but not like my dad described—not with unfinished business. Think about it. In the whole story, who is it that got the worst deal? Who is it that was executed for a crime he didn't commit?"

All of a sudden it was obvious. And I was going to say it, too—*the cat*. But I never got the chance, and neither did Yasmeen. This time it wasn't some puny draft but an Arctic blast that shot through the attic, kicking the leaves and dust into a whirlwind as turbulent as a minitornado, knocking the boxes around so that they wobbled, they clattered, they fell and broke open. Then there was a flash of blue-green light, a crack like cannon fire, and finally a howl like the most enormous cat in the universe had had its tail pinched by the most enormous rocking chair.

The whole thing lasted only a few seconds, but it was an overwhelming few seconds, and after the dust and leaves had settled, after the light had returned to its usual dimness, after the howling's echo had subsided—we three were left looking at each other, blinking, our pulses racing.

When I could breathe—and my heart had slowed to something like normal—I said, "I think you're right, Mr. Blanco. I think, as of now, the ghost is gone for good."

Chapter Thirty-six

Walking home from the Harvey house, Yasmeen had a goofy idea. "Let's go visit Marianne," she said, "and stouthearted Floyd. Let's pay our respects."

"Not St. Bernard's," I whined, "not again."

"Oh, come on. After all, today's All Saints Day! The first of November—the Day of the Dead in Latin American countries, the day you honor the ancestors."

"How do you *know* this stuff?" I asked.

Yasmeen shrugged. "You pick up a lot when you read the encyclopedia. Hurry now— I'll race ya."

"I hate racing!" But I took off running, anyway.

A few minutes later, all out of breath, we were standing in front of Marianne Harvey's grumpy angel at St. Bernard's cemetery. Yasmeen nodded at the markers. "The inscriptions make sense now," she said. "Gilmore Harvey must have written them. He *was* trying to tell us something."

I read the two stones again. Gilmore Harvey's: SO SHALL THE RIGHTEOUS ESCAPE THE GRAVE.

And Marianne's: IN DEATH, THE ETERNAL WIFE.

Yasmeen sighed. "It's all so sad, like Romeo and Juliet." Her voice sounded peculiar, so I looked over. Wouldn't you know there was a tear on her cheek? I shook my head, disgusted. Girls, I thought.

Then I tried to talk, and my voice came out sounding like a frog. "We know it's you down there, Floyd. Rest in peace, pal."

I called Dad from Yasmeen's. "Be home at five-thirty," he told me. "Oh—and bring Yasmeen, why don't you? I've . . . uh, I've got something I need to give her."

Hanging out at the Popps is not usually that fun, because they don't even have video games and all the snacks are healthy. But—honestly? I was trying to avoid cleaning the basement. Usually I wouldn't mind that much, but now I was feeling sort of cheated. I mean, we had hardly gotten to trick-or-treat, I was going to wind up paying for the baby monitor out of my own savings, and worst of all, nobody seemed to care that we had solved the great catnapping caper.

My house was really quiet when Yasmeen and I walked through the front door.

"Luau?" I called. "Dad? Mom?"

I looked at Yasmeen, and she shrugged.

"Hello?" I called again.

"Hello?" my dad's voice answered. "That you, kids? I'm in the basement. Bring down the mop and you can help me with this floor, okay?"

Great. He had saved me a grungy job, just like Mom promised.

The mop was in the closet at the top of the

basement stairs. "You don't have to help," I told Yasmeen. "It's not your basement."

"I don't mind," she said.

"How come there aren't any lights on down here?" Dragging the mop behind me, I felt my way down the stairs. "Dad?" I called. "How come there aren't any—"

"Oh, you want *lights!*" Dad said, and with that they flashed on, illuminating our totally clean basement, which contained all our neighbors on Chickadee Court, plus Kyle and Cammie and Officer Krichels and a bunch more people I couldn't even take in at once—all under a big banner that read, CONGRATULATIONS, SUPERSLEUTHS!

It is lucky that even though I am not the world's toughest kid, my heart is pretty strong. Otherwise it would have stopped cold. That's how shocked I was.

With everyone watching and smiling and making thumbs-up signs, I looked over at my best friend who happens to be a girl. "Yasmeen?" I said.

She was grinning. "What do you know?" she said. "They do care after all."

It was a good party. There was a big cake with a picture of a black cat on it in frosting. My dad was wearing his new glasses, which my mom said made him look distinguished, but he said made him look old. I met Boopsie. She had drool all over her face and her eyes kept crossing. Mr. Lee was holding her, and seeing him reminded me that for a while I had thought he might be the catnapper—mostly because some instinct told me he was suspicious. It was instinct that had made Yasmeen mistrust Kyle, too, I remembered. It seemed like maybe sometimes instinct steered you pretty far wrong.

Anyway, Mr. Lee offered to let me hold Boopsie, but I said, no thanks, I couldn't hold a new baby and a mop at the same time. "Did you name her yet?" I asked.

Mr. Lee smiled. "Yes, we did, and I hope you're pleased."

"Me? Why would I be pleased? I mean, I'm sure you picked a good name and—"

"*Alex,*" Mr. Lee said.

"Yes?" I said.

Mr. Lee laughed. "No, I mean Alex is what we've named her."

"How sweet!" Yasmeen said.

"Sweet," I echoed, and I tried to smile, but really I didn't think the neighborhood needed another Alex, especially a drooling girl Alex who couldn't even keep her eyes pointed the same direction.

"Don't worry." Bub had been standing behind me, and now he spoke so Mr. Lee couldn't hear. "I don't think anybody's gonna get the two of you confused."

Sophie was at the party, too, of course. Everybody was congratulating her on being so clever and brave, which she deserved I guess. But it didn't make her any less obnoxious. She had brought the baby monitor with her, closed up in its original box again. She said we could take it back to Best Buy-Buy now.

"You mean it works like it used to?" I asked. "That is so great. I thought I was going to have to pay for it."

"Oh, yeah, it works," Sophie said, "better than ever."

"What do you mean 'better than ever'?" Yasmeen asked.

Sophie reached into her jeans pocket and pulled out a handful of metal pieces. "I couldn't figure out where these ones were supposed to go, so I left them out," she said. "Probably they weren't that important. Only now besides cell phone conversations, the receiver picks up TV, too—soap operas and talk shows and junk. That makes it better than a plain old baby monitor, my mom says. My mom says the company ought to pay me for improving it. I wonder how much they'll pay me? My mom says she'll write a letter—"

Yasmeen and I left her and went to get punch. I don't think she cared that we were gone. She turned to poor Mrs. Blanco, who happened to be standing there, and kept right on talking.

"I'll help you pay for the baby monitor," Yasmeen said.

"Thanks," I said. Then I dipped her a Styrofoam cup of punch, and she dipped me one, and we held our cups up and touched them together. It was a toast except we didn't say anything. We didn't have to. I was going to take a drink when I felt something brush between my legs. Something that was furry and had a tail.

"Oh, sorry, Luau. Didn't mean to leave you out," I said.

"Does he even like punch?" Yasmeen asked me.

"He likes tuna juice."

"It's not the same thing," Yasmeen said.

"Either way, we should toast him, too," I said. "I guess now you'll admit that cats can be pretty good explainers."

"What do you mean?" Yasmeen asked.

"I mean it was Luau who told us where Halloween was," I said.

"Get out!" she said. "It was dumb feline luck!"

I tried being calm and reasonable. "Think about it, Yasmeen. Why were we hearing Arnold's wheel in the first place? Luau went over

by the hamster cage on purpose.   knew somebody would recognize that noise."

Yasmeen gave me a look.

"You don't believe me? Let's ask him," I said.
"Luau, did you lead us to Miss Deirdre on purpose?"

Luau sat down, swiped a paw over his right
ear, and swished his tail.

I shrugged. "There you have it."

"Have *what*?" Yasmeen said.

"He says he did it on purpose. He says he
knew Jeremiah was trick-or-treating with us, and
he knew Jeremiah would recognize that noise."

Yasmeen rolled her eyes. "Ask him if it was on
purpose that he picked such a totally wacko
owner who thinks he can talk to cats!" she said.

"Okay," I said. "Luau, was it on purpose that
you picked such a totally wacko owner who
thinks he can talk to cats?"

But Luau was too impatient to continue the
conversation. He just looked at me and blinked,
which was Luau's way of saying *ha-ha*.